Praise for the Raine Stockton Dog Mystery Series

"An exciting, original and suspense-laden whodunit... A simply fabulous mystery starring a likeable, dedicated heroine..."
--*Midwest Book Review*

"A delightful protagonist...a well-crafted mystery."
--*Romantic Times*

"There can't be too many golden retrievers in mystery fiction for my taste."
--*Deadly Pleasures*

" An intriguing heroine, a twisty tale, a riveting finale, and a golden retriever to die for. [This book] will delight mystery fans and enchant dog lovers."
---*Carolyn Hart*

"Has everything--wonderful characters, surprising twists, great dialogue. Donna Ball knows dogs, knows the Smoky Mountains, and knows how to write a page turner. I loved it."
--*Beverly Connor*

"Very entertaining… combines a likeable heroine and a fascinating mystery… a story of suspense with humor and tenderness."
--*Carlene Thompson*

Books in the Raine Stockton Dog Mystery series:

RAPID FIRE

A Raine Stockton Dog Mystery

Donna Ball

www.donnaball.net

cover by Sapphire Dreams

Published by Blue Merle Publishing
Drawer H
Mountain City Georgia 30562
www.bluemerlepublishing.com

ISBN- 978-0-9857748-5-1

This book is also available in digital format for your e-reader.

Previously published in mass market paperback by Signet Books

First Blue Merle printing January 2013

Chapter One

There is a cliché that every boy who has ever been to high school knows: If you're looking for a wild time, your best bet is the preacher's daughter. Well, if you think she's trouble, you ought to check out the judge's daughter.

That would be me.

Even though my father has been dead for years, and even though I am a full-grown woman who has been away to college and opened her own business and been married and everything, most people still think of me not as Raine Stockton, Grown-up Woman, but as Judge Stockton's daughter. That's what happens when you live in the same small community all your life—it's hard to get away from your past. And, like most kids who, for whatever reason, are held to a higher standard than others, I guess I always felt I had a lot of past to get away from.

I don't mean to imply that I was promiscuous as a teenager. I'm sure I didn't have any more fun than any other girl in a county whose full-time population is less than three thousand, whose county seat doesn't have a movie theater, roller rink or bowling alley, and whose Saturday-night entertainment options are decidedly limited, if you know what I mean. The teen pregnancy rate is quite a bit above the national average in our little corner of the Smoky Mountains, but I'm happy to say I beat those odds.

The truth of the matter is, I've really loved only two men in my whole life, and I fell in love with both of them in high school. The first one grew up to be deputy sheriff and a sterling asset to our little community of Hansonville, North Carolina. The second spent more time in trouble with the law than out of it and has now been a fugitive from justice for more than ten years. Guess which one I married.

Wrong. I actually married Deputy Sheriff Buck Lawson. In fact, I married him twice. And most days I'm still not certain I made the right choice.

Currently Buck and I live apart, although we haven't quite gotten around to untying the knot for the second—and most likely, the last—time. For one thing, it's all too embarrassing. First you're married; then you're not; then you're married again. No one likes to make a mistake, but to keep making it over and over again—that just makes you look like you haven't been paying attention. For another thing…well, I suppose that "other thing," which neither one of us can quite put into words, is the real reason we stay married even though we can't bring ourselves to live together.

As for Andy, the one who got away— literally—he was actually one of the reasons my marriage started to fray the first time. But it's not what you might think. Approximately six months after Buck and I were married, the local headquarters of a petrochemical plant was bombed, and four people died. Buck, along with a good portion of the known world and every federal officer who cared to go on record, thought Andy was guilty. I thought he was innocent. It's never good for a couple to discover that early in a marriage how passionately they can disagree over something so fundamental, and when the argument is over an old boyfriend... Well, as I said, that's never good. Perhaps even worse is the fact that we never got to find out which one of us was right. Andy Fontana outwitted both the local and federal authorities and fled the country before he could be arrested. In the process he became something of a folk hero. No one has ever seen or heard from him since.

Until, that is, the first day of summer 2006, the year I call my Summer of the Bear.

In the middle of the morning on that day, I was doing one of my favorite things in the world: practically nothing. Cisco, my golden retriever, and I were lounging on the cabin porch of the ranger station in the high woods of the Nantahala Forest, watching Rick Anderson put together an educational diorama composed of a stuffed red fox, raccoon, hawk and copperhead snake. It is worth noting that all the creatures—except perhaps the copperhead—had died of natural causes and had then been expertly, almost too realistically, prepared for this display by a local taxidermist. I have worked with animals all my life, but I still found it a little unnerving to watch

Rick kneeling there in front of the glass case with a snake under one arm And a hawk under the other.

"You need to put the fox on the rock, not the raccoon," I advised. "And put some bushes up there behind him. You know a fox isn't going to be standing out in the open like that, away from cover. Especially not in broad daylight."

"You want to come over here and do this yourself, Raine?" Rick wriggled his big arm into the display case to place the raccoon, knocking the fox askew in the process.

I was leaning back in the rocking chair with my feet propped on the porch rail, sipping Mr. Pibb and munching on salted peanuts from a cellophane bag, and the last thing I wanted to do was get up and go anywhere. "No, thanks, I can supervise from here."

Technically, Rick was my boss, but since technically I didn't actually start working for him for another five days, I could enjoy razzing him a little. Besides, our little group at the Long Branch Ranger Station was an informal bunch, close-knit and easygoing, and no one stood on ceremony much. We were all spread too thin and paid too little to do the job for any other reason than that we loved it.

There aren't a whole lot of employment opportunities in a rural Smoky Mountain community for a girl fresh out of college with a degree in wildlife science, but as it happened, when I got out of college I was far more interested in becoming Mrs. Buck Lawson than I was in looking for a job. By the time I was ready to go to work—no, begging to go work—it wasn't my degree that got me a job with the local forest service, but my dog.

That's right, my dog. Oh, I know my father pulled a few strings to keep me in the county, but the fact is that by then I had already made something of a name for myself in the search and rescue world with my tracking dog, Cassidy (who just happens to be Cisco's grandmother). And since any job that's located on the edge of one of the state's great wilderness areas is, by nature, going to involve a certain amount of search and rescue, I really was a natural.

Unfortunately, the funding for my full-time position ran out a few years back, and I was reassigned to the "temporary, part-time" category. That means I come in three days a week during peak tourist season and fill in for the full-timers when they're away on vacation, and occasionally I'm called in as a "consultant"—on temporary, part-timer's wages—when there's an emergency or a natural disaster or some other situation in which a wildlife science degree is not quite as valuable as a willing pair of hands. I still do search and rescue work, but with a new dog now, since Cassidy died a hero three years ago. And usually, these days, I don't get paid for it.

The truth of the matter is, I kind of like the way things turned out. I manage to support myself and my canine family with the boarding kennel and dog-training business I opened after I inherited my parents' house and the forty-eight acres that were attached to it, and even though the part-time work with the forest service doesn't pay much, I enjoy being back with the guys a few times a year, bouncing around in the jeep, doing what I love— or even, as is more often the case, sitting behind the counter handing out maps to tourists. And they let me bring my dog to work.

Cisco, the dog in question, opened one big brown eye hopefully when he heard the cellophane peanut bag rattle, but he wasn't hopeful enough to lift his head from its comfortable position between his paws. I ignored his baleful, one-eyed gaze, and with a huffy sigh, he sank back into sleep.

"The thing is," I explained to Rick, popping another peanut into my mouth, "what you're trying to do here is capture what they call a 'defining moment'—you know, like a freeze-frame in a movie. The whole predator-prey thing. You got your hawk swooping down on the fox. The fox eyeing the raccoon. And the raccoon is just about to put his foot down on the snake. Now, that's drama. That's excitement. That's storytelling. It's the whole circle of life."

Rick gave me a dark look as he stretched behind the case to try to right the fox, the left side of his face flattened against the glass. "I'll give you circle of life," he muttered. The fox tipped over at the touch of his groping fingers, followed by the raccoon, followed by a pile of artfully arranged broken sticks and twigs, where, I presumed, he had planned to place the snake. While he cursed, the phone inside the building began to ring.

"Damn it, Raine, get on over here and put this thing together. You're littler than I am and it won't take you but a minute to get this stuff in here."

I chuckled and finished off my drink. "Sorry. That sounds to me like a job for a full time-employee." I crumpled up the peanut bag and swung my feet to the floor. Cisco immediately got to all fours, tail wagging, grinning expectantly. "Tell you what I'll do, though," I added as I started toward the door. "I'll get the phone for you on my way to the trash can."

"Yeah, well, bring me that roll of baling wire when you come back out, will you?"

The screen door creaked and Cisco followed me into the cool, dark interior. The room was just big enough to hold a U-shaped counter, a display rack with maps and brochures, and a table featuring regional souvenirs—sorghum syrup and chow-chow in mason jars, a basket of hand-carved wooden whistles, and some books about local attractions. The walls were paneled in rough-cut cedar, and the crisp, green scent of the woods filled the air.

I slipped behind the counter and caught the phone on the fifth ring. "Ranger station."

"Who is this?" a breathless, rather querulous female voice demanded. Before I could answer she rushed on. "This is Caralee Tucker, out on Valley Street, and I want y'all to come down here and get this bear that's been tearing up my husband's workshop."

I said quickly, "Is the bear still there, Mrs. Tucker?"

"No, he's not still there! Do you think I'd be wasting time talking on the phone with you if he was still there? Joe chased him off with a garden hoe and he took off down the road toward Vince Miller's place. But you should've seen the mess he made! Burlap sacks shredded like newspaper, toolboxes turned over, nuts and bolts everywhere; tore ever' bit of stuffing out of an old mattress we had stored down there and smashed an aluminum trash can flat, I tell you! Birdseed scattered from one end of the yard to the other!"

Ah, birdseed. So that was what he was after. I smiled a little as I said, "Do you keep your birdseed stored in the workshop, Mrs. Tucker?"

"Not anymore, we don't! It's scattered from here to high water!"

"Well, try to keep it stored in a sealed container next time, and it might be a good idea to put your feeders away for a little while. Sometimes when a bear finds an easy source of food like your birdseed, he's tempted to come back and make a pest of himself."

"Pest! *Pest!* She sputtered out the word like it was in a foreign language. "A pest is mealy worms on your tomatoes, young lady, or black flies at the church supper. This bear was five hundred pounds if he was an ounce and he wrecked my husband's workshop! And I can tell you for a fact he won't be coming back here to make a pest of himself because you are going to come down here and get him right this minute!"

Cisco chose that moment to put his front paws on the counter and investigate the possibility of a dropped crumb or two. Like the bear, he was highly food motivated. I rapped the countertop sharply with my fingernail and said, "Off!" With something less than lightning speed—there was, after all, a sprinkling of powdered sugar left over from Rick's morning donut scattered across the counter—Cisco complied. Caralee Tucker screeched in my ear, "What? What did you say?"

I winced apologetically but didn't think Mrs. Tucker was in the mood for me to explain that I had been talking to a dog and not to her. I said, "A five-hundred-pound bear would be highly unusual this time of year, Mrs. Tucker, and at any rate, I'm sure he's headed back for the woods where he came from. We've found that in these situations it's usually best not to interfere—"

"Do you mean you're not going to do anything? Decent citizens are terrorized by bears in their own home and you're not going to do a thing?"

"Well, of course, if it becomes a nuisance—"

"Nuisance?" I actually had to take the receiver away from my ear that time, and even Cisco's ears pricked up at the decibel level of the shriek. "You don't call destroying thousands of dollars worth of personal property a *nuisance!"*

I could see this was going nowhere, so I said, "Whereabouts on Valley Street do you live, Mrs. Tucker?"

I copied down the address and the phone number, and I told her, "I can't promise somebody will be out there today, but we'll do what we can, okay? In the meantime, if you see the bear again, please don't confront him or try to chase him with a hoe. Black bears are usually pretty shy animals, but you don't want to put him in a situation where he has to defend himself."

When I came back on the porch, Rick had gotten the fox back on its feet but had given up on the raccoon and opted for a soft drink from the vending machine instead. He had also taken over my rocking chair. The hawk he had left carelessly on the floor, wings splayed, talons curled, flat on its back.

Cisco, being a bird dog, spotted this immediately. His ears shot forward, his hackles went up, and he sank to his belly, preparing to spring. I said sharply, "Cisco, leave it," and scooped the dead bird off the floor approximately two seconds before the carefully preserved hawk—and the taxpayers' money—was reduced to a cloud of flying feathers. The key to being a good dog trainer is to never—I mean never—take your eye off your dog. Especially when your dog has as little impulse control as Cisco does.

I placed the hawk carefully on top of the display case where it belonged and wondered what Rick had done with the snake. I spotted it on the swing, which was the only other available sitting area, and my lips turned down wryly. His idea of a joke, I supposed.

I watched as Cisco approached the hawk, stiff legged, nose extended, and sniffed. He looked abashed and began to wag his tail slowly when he realized that the creature was not, after all, a bird, and I grinned and scratched his ear. "Easy mistake, fellow," I said.

I removed the snake from the swing and placed it on the rail in front of Rick, nodding toward the room from which I had come, and said, "Bear."

"So I heard."

"I wrote the information on the pad by the phone. It was out on Valley Street."

He grunted and drank from the can.

I frowned a little. "Seems odd, don't you think, a bear coming out of the hills that close to town?"

Rick looked at me with the soda can halfway to his lips and his brows raised. "What hills?" he said flatly. "You've seen what they're doing to the mountain over behind Valley Street. If you were a bear, would you stay there?"

My lips compressed and I nodded glumly. This was not exactly a neutral subject with me. The front side of the mountain that was currently being shaved off to make room for modern development faced Valley Street. The back side of that same mountain looked down over my house. "Yeah, well, I guess this won't be the first wildlife complaint like that we get this year," I agreed in a dispirited tone.

"Or the next, or the next. Those animals have got to go somewhere. Like you said, the circle of life." He drank from the can again and jerked his head toward the diorama. "Sure you don't want to make yourself useful with that thing?"

"Knock yourself out." I tossed the reel of baling wire to him, and he caught it one-handed. "I'm teaching a class this afternoon. Gotta pay the rent somehow."

Rick turned an imploring gaze to Cisco. "How about you, boy? Want to hang out and give ole Uncle Rick a hand?" He patted his chest invitingly.

Before I could stop him, Cisco happily flung himself onto Rick's lap. The rocking chair overbalanced and soft drink sprayed everywhere as Rick, wildly flailing his arms and legs, tried to right himself. I shouted, "Cisco, *off*" and Cisco, as graceful as a baby elephant, sprang to the ground. Rick jumped up, scrubbing sticky soda off his uniform and rubbing the places where Cisco's nails had dug into his chest.

I grabbed Cisco's collar. "Sorry about that," I muttered, chagrined. "But you *did* ask for it." And the truth is, even the great ones can't watch their dogs *every* minute.

Rick looked at me with absolutely no humor in his face. "Let me get this straight. You make your living as a dog trainer?"

I said, equally deadpan, "See you next week, Rick. Cisco, let's go."

Chapter Two

The spring had been hot and dry, and the fire hazard notice on the Smokey the Bear sign in front of the ranger station read HIGH. But no one without the aid of the sign would have guessed it. The undergrowth was lush and green and as thick as I had ever seen it, and word had come down from the higher-ups about doing a controlled burn later in the year to clear out what I called "trash growth" and to revitalize the soil. I hoped my temporary stint was over by then. Necessary as they are, there is nothing fun about working a burn.

I left the still, lush greens of forty-two-hundred-foot elevation for the hotter, brighter and more populated regions below, taking my time and enjoying the ride. In my part of the world you are either in the heart of the mountain or surrounded by mountains wherever you go; they are big, round, blue-shadowed matrons, or tangled green woodlands roaring with waterfalls, or purple-layered peaks and undulations highlighted with green and gold as far as the eye can see. On my way back to civilization I passed through all three kinds of mountain views, and each one, as always, was more exhilarating than the last.

I lowered the back window a little so that Cisco, safely secured in his canine seat belt, could enjoy the same view with his nose that I did with my eyes. He panted happily, drinking it all in.

Hanover County, in the heart of the Smoky Mountains, always experiences a population surge in the summer and fall. It's something we locals, who wear our badges of winter survival with a kind of casual smugness, have learned to tolerate without too much complaint. The "damned tourists," after all, account for seventy percent of the year-end average of most small businesses in town, and without them, I venture to say, the forest service wouldn't have much need for part-time employees like, well, me.

A few of those tourists fall in love with the place and decide to stay; they build summerhouses or, in some cases, full-time retirement homes. The summer people are a nuisance, but they do add to the tax base, I suppose, and we figure that by the time those who have decided to "retire" here have made it through three winters they deserve the right to be called permanent. Of course, not many of them do.

Around the middle of May we start getting the first few bedraggled hikers off the Appalachian Trail, and by the first of June the Land Rovers and the Cadillacs can be seen parked in front of Miss Meg's Cafe on Main Street. But it's usually the Fourth of July before you have to wait as much as two minutes to make a left turn onto Highway 97, unless, of course, there's a shift change at the textile plant. Here it was barely noon on a Wednesday, and I had to wait for at least a dozen cars to go by before I could make my turn.

That was depressing.

The shortest route to get back to my house was through the small downtown area of Hansonville—three red lights, one at each block, a handful of retail shops, and the big, old sprawling Hansonville Inn, established 1832, that dominated the corner of Main and Mountain streets. I wasn't surprised to notice another FOR SALE sign in the window of the inn. Even with a good tourist season, it's hard to keep a place like that running year-round.

And this appeared to be shaping up to be a stellar tourist season. Every spot in front of Miss Meg's Cafe was filled, which nixed my idea of stopping by and asking Meg to wrap up one of her chicken-fried steak sandwiches to go. There were plenty of faces on the street I didn't recognize. I had to stop short to allow a mud-splashed SUV in a hurry to back out of a parking space, and it wasn't until I noticed three or four Mexican workers leaning against a pickup truck at the side of the building that I started to put the pieces together. These weren't all tourists. A lot of them were construction workers.

One of the Mexican workers spotted Cisco, who had his nose and as much of his furry face as he could get pressed through the crack of the window, and he grinned and nudged his friends, pointing. They said something in Spanish I couldn't understand, and I tried to smile at them as I drove by. If I had been that far away from my family and friends and pets, in a place where I didn't even speak the language, the sight of a golden retriever would have made me grin too.

I pulled into the Feed and Seed at the edge of town, checked my watch and decided there would be no time for visiting today. "Stay here," I told Cisco and rolled the window the rest of the way down as I jumped out of the Explorer.

Jeff Hawkins special-orders dog food for me, an ultra-premium brand that isn't sold much this side of Asheville. I know he doesn't make any profit on it, so I always try to do as much of my shopping in his store as I can—leashes, harnesses, fencing materials, things like that. I also like to hang around and talk dogs with him— he breeds championship German shorthaired pointers—but today there wasn't time.

He was in the middle of a conversation with Dexter Franklin when I came in, and it didn't look like a very happy exchange. I heard Dexter say something about "goddamned ruination of this county," and Jeff was agreeing mildly, "I hear you, Dex; I hear you." But Jeff looked relieved when he saw me.

"Hey, there, Miss Raine. Got your order in just this morning."

"Hi, Jeff," I greeted him. "I've got Cisco in the car, so I'm going to have to grab it and run."

"I'll get it right out."

My memories of the Feed and Seed go back to childhood, and I always love coming here. It smells of oats and horse leather and, faintly, of the ashes from the wood stove that burns all day during the winter. Today the doors were open and a cool, sunny breeze wafted through, and I wished

I didn't have to hurry.

"Hi, Mr. Franklin." While Jeff went to the back room to haul out the dog food, I leaned on the counter and started writing the check. "How's it going?"

Dexter Franklin slapped his camouflage cap atop his balding head, muttered something unintelligible and stalked out. A moment later I heard the door of his pickup slam and tires splattering gravel as he peeled out of the parking lot. Jeff, emerging from the back room with his arms stretched out by two forty-pound bags of dog food, gave me a wry look.

"What's eating him?" I asked, nodding toward the door by which Dexter had just left as I tore the check out of the checkbook.

"Ah, you know." Jeff carried the bags awkwardly toward the car and I hurried to open up the back for him. "He thought he was going to get the grading contract for that road they're cutting through on Hawk Mountain, and it turns out those city folk double-crossed him. Brought in their own outfit to do the job."

"No kidding." I was unable to keep a rather pleased note of surprise out of my tone. "I always thought the only reason he approved the construction permit was because he was promised the job." Did I mention that Dexter Franklin is one of our three county commissioners?

"Yeah, well, you dance with the devil…"

"You're bound to get burned," I finished for him and grinned as I edged past him toward my car.

It was then that I noticed that someone was standing next to it, and I quickened my step. Not only was someone standing beside my car; he was petting my dog.

First, a word to the wise: Don't *ever* go up to a vehicle and start petting a strange dog, even if that dog is doing his best to wriggle his whole body through the window in an absolute ecstasy of invitation. Some dogs can become very territorial when in a car and may feel the need to defend that territory with their teeth. And although Cisco was obviously not one of those dogs, I *was* one of those owners. I don't like anyone messing with my dogs when I'm not around, especially a stranger.

However, I do believe in giving people the benefit of the doubt, so instead of shouting, "Back off, fool!" I called out, "Hi!" in as friendly a tone as I could manage as I made my way forward.

When the man turned from his vigorous rubbing of Cisco's ears, the very activity that was apparently causing my usually devoted dog to give up all thoughts of home and hearth in favor of flinging himself at this stranger's feet, I recognized the construction worker who had been so happy to see Cisco hanging out of the window when we drove past a few minutes ago.

He didn't look much over thirty, and he was dressed neatly for a construction worker in faded jeans and a plaid shirt that was open at the throat. I couldn't help noticing the gold crucifix he wore around his neck, mostly because you don't often see necklaces on men around here. The grin that split his face was as broad now as it had been then.

"Pretty dog," he said. "Fine dog." His Spanish accent was thick and his English vocabulary obviously limited, but he knew the only words he needed to make friends with me.

I smiled and relaxed as I opened the back hatch for Jeff. "He sure seems to like you."

Jeff set the bags of dog food inside the truck, and Cisco barely even noticed. He put a paw on top of the window and begged for more ear rubs. The stranger kindly obliged.

"I have dog like this," he said. "At home."

"You have a golden retriever?" I asked.

"Yellow dog," he agreed. "Fine dog."

I thanked Jeff and closed the hatchback.

"You take care, now," Jeff said. He gave a friendly nod to the stranger as he came around the car and added, "Bye, Mr. Cisco. Try not to eat it all at once."

I took out my keys. "My dog's name is Cisco," I explained. Then I pointed to my own chest. "I'm Raine." He returned the favor by pointing to his chest. "Manny." I grinned. "Nice to meet you. Cisco thinks so too."

"Cisco," said the stranger, giving the dog's ears a final rub before he stepped away from the car. He pronounced it "Seesko," which I rather liked. "Is good name. Good dog."

"Thanks," I said and slid into the driver's seat. "I hope you get to see your own dog soon," I added before I closed the door.

The man smiled and nodded, and he was still smiling as I drove off.

My route home took me down Valley Street, where the first phase of construction had begun on the access road that would strip a swath across the mountain to allow utility lines to be laid. The good news was that the lines would be underground, which is really the only practical way to supply telephone and electrical service in a remote mountain region like this. The bad news was that the scar that was being gouged into the face of the mountain would never completely heal.

This was all preparatory to a proposed resort community that was being brought to our mountaintop courtesy of a development group in Atlanta. The first step, apparently, was to secure the infrastructure, which began on this side of the mountain with utilities, and would continue on my side of the mountain with access roads. If the defoliation of Valley Street was any indication of what lay in store, I was in no hurry for the next stage of the project to get under way.

I felt that familiar tightening in my stomach as I rounded the corner and saw the bare, red hillside where mountain laurel used to grow. There were a couple of big, yellow bulldozers parked at the bottom of the hill, and another one was roaring and pushing its way up the mountainside while dusty red dump trucks lumbered down a path so steep I actually cringed to watch them. I noticed Dexter Franklin's truck parked near one of the idle bulldozers. He was talking and gesticulating emphatically to a man in a hard hat.

More power to you, Dexter, I thought grimly as I eased my way past. If it wasn't for you and your buddies on the commission, we wouldn't be in this mess.

I kept my eyes open for a bear as I negotiated my way through the noise and the diesel fumes of Valley Street, but I never saw a sign of him. I wasn't surprised. Like Rick had said, if you were a bear, would you stay here?

Chapter Three

At Dog Daze Boarding and Training Facility the summer months are our busiest time of year, making it a feast-or-famine situation as far as my employment goes. Although we do have indoor training facilities for use during inclement weather, the students who are my bread and butter often travel as much as two hours to take a class, and in the wintertime that's just not practical. So I try to make up for it by offering more classes during the months of the year when the roads are clear.

On Wednesday afternoon, which this was, we have day classes for those lucky dogs whose owners get Wednesdays off—a fairly common practice in small towns like this—or who don't have to work at all. We offer Puppy Manners and the Family Dog from one to two o'clock, both of which are basic obedience courses for the family pet and are always filled. Then, at two thirty, we start with what I call the fun stuff: continuing obedience, where the dogs learn to heel off leash, jump and retrieve; and agility, which is my specialty.

The other half of the "we" in Dog Daze is Maude Braselton, my partner in the business. Maude worked for my father, the judge, until he retired, and has been a part of the family for as long as I can remember. She taught me everything I know about dogs and was the only one who gave me any encouragement when I came up with the crazy idea to open a dog-training school out here in the middle of nowhere.

When I came rushing in at ten till one, Maude was in the office, printing out homework sheets for the obedience classes. Every year we get one or two people who think that obedience school is like first grade—you send your dog there for an hour a week, and they come home trained. Long ago, we decided to make it easy on everyone and send home written instructions every week to tell people what *they* have to do to train their dogs.

"Is there anything to eat?" I demanded without preamble. "All I had was a bag of peanuts this morning and I didn't have time to stop for lunch. You should have seen the crowd in town. Hey, the parking lot looks pretty good, by the way, for the third week of class. We may have picked up a few of the no-shows from last week."

The dropout rate is one of the banes of dog training and can often be as high as sixty percent by the fourth week of a six-week class. Whenever I saw our parking lot (a loose term to describe the partially graveled area between the side of my house and the fenced agility field) three-quarters filled midway through a course, I always got a surge of ego. It meant we were doing something right.

Maude slid open the top drawer of the desk and tossed me a Snickers bar. Cisco, being a retriever, launched himself onto his hind legs and tried to snatch it out of the air, but fortunately I was faster than he was—this time.

"Baby Face is back," Maude said.

I had peeled back the wrapper and was preparing to take a huge bite of the candy bar, but Maude's words stopped me in the act. "Oh, goody," I said and couldn't even manage to feign enthusiasm.

On the subject of dropouts, Baby Face was a dog I almost would have paid not to return. Of course, no dog trainer wishes ill to one of her students, and it wasn't his fault he was such a terror, but if ever a dog did not need to be in a class situation, it was him. Every week I begged his owner to take him out of class and put him in our board-and-train program, and every week, no matter how minutely I explained the process, she looked at me blankly.

Furthermore, if I could ever find the person who sold a Jack Russell terrier puppy to an eighty-two-year-old woman, there would be more than a few harsh words exchanged, I can promise you that.

On the first day of Puppy Manners class, Baby Face had dragged his frail, white-haired, Band-Aid-covered owner across the threshold of the puppy room, pawing the air and barking nonstop. Before class was over he had started two dogfights and had bitten me on the arm. A general rule of thumb for children and dogs: If you want to do well in class, don't bite the teacher on the first day of school.

Moreover, his owner was either extremely hard of hearing or had some cognitive dysfunction. She didn't follow a single instruction in class, could never remember where she put her treats and didn't seem to understand that homework was something to be practiced every single day at home with your dog. When she had not shown up for class last week I had assumed that the frustration had become as intense for her as it was for me and that she wouldn't be coming back.

I carefully folded the wrapper back over the candy bar and tucked it into my shirt pocket. "Well," I said, squaring my shoulders, "I guess I'd better get in there."

"You needn't look so grim," Maude said. "You're not an infantryman preparing to take Pork Chop Hill."

Maude was a sixtyish woman, lean and tan with short white hair and a crisp British accent that made every word she uttered seem charged with import and authority. Today she wore a starched white sleeveless shirt with a button-down collar and pressed khaki trousers, the very picture of businesslike efficiency, and exactly the kind of person I would want for an instructor if I were taking a dog-training class. In view of my rumpled denim shorts, faded Golden Retriever Club of America T-shirt, and unbuttoned striped overshirt, it was easy to see who was head trainer in our facility.

I paused at the door to give Maude a dark look of warning. "Joke all you like," I told her, "but if Baby Face ever makes it out of puppy kindergarten, he'll be in *your* class next."

And, with a stoic breath, I marched off to face the music.

Today, instead of the hot dogs and cheese cubes I recommended everyone use as training treats, Mrs. Foster—Baby Face's owner—had brought pretzels and chocolate chip cookies. When I tried to explain to her that, in addition to chocolate being toxic to dogs, the sugar in the cookies would be extremely bad for Baby Face's teeth, she argued, "But you said to bring human treats. I heard you say that. Didn't you hear her say that, Henry?"

Henry, her sixty-year-old son, drove her to class and spent the hour sitting in one of the orange plastic spectator chairs that edged the room, looking sour and disgruntled. In response to his mother's question, he grunted and folded his arms across his chest.

I compromised by letting her keep the pretzels, and the first thing I knew Baby Face had drawn blood by trying to snatch a pretzel out of his owner's hand. Out came the first aid kit and the incident report, and class was ten minutes late getting started.

All in all, though, things went pretty smoothly. I had to unwind Mrs. Foster from her dog's leash only once, and the four-month-old malamute who had been pulling at the leash ever since it was introduced surprised me by heeling in perfect step with its owner around the room. All in all, I was feeling pretty pleased with myself as I dismissed the puppy class and hurried to set up for agility.

The best thing about puppy class is that it's inside, in the air-conditioning. Eighty-four degrees in the three o'clock sun can be hard on humans *and* dogs when you're both running as fast as you can, and unless it was pouring down rain, agility class was always held outside.

I had thirty minutes between classes to set up and organize my thoughts. I grabbed my slightly squashed Snickers bar, shed the long-sleeved shirt, and paused to wrap my knee before heading for the door. I had had surgery on the knee earlier in the year and, even though it was doing fine now, I had a big competition in Asheville coming up in three days, and I wasn't about to take a chance on re-injuring it.

One of my students had given me a cap with I RUN NAKED embroidered on the crown, and I snatched it up on the way out, stuffing my unruly dark curls up under it. The caption isn't as risqué as it sounds. It simply refers to the fact that in most agility organizations dogs are required to run without their collars—or naked, as we say. Still, the slogan "I Run Naked" is too good to resist, and agility competitors have a lot of fun with it.

I said good-bye to departing students and hello to arriving ones as I made my way outside, trying to surreptitiously scarf down the Snickers bar on my way. I freed Cisco from his holding pen—he really was nothing but a nuisance in puppy class—and made him heel with me, aided by the lure of a greasy bit of hot dog, all the way to the agility field.

I was just turning to latch the gate when I saw the sheriff's patrol car coming down the dusty drive.

Most people know about my relationship with the sheriff's department—both personal and professional—but for those who don't, having a patrol car pull up in front of one's place of business is not exactly the best advertisement. And on our busiest day, right in the middle of the change of classes, Buck's unexpected visit was doing nothing but creating a traffic jam.

I tried not to let my annoyance show as I left the agility field to meet him, gulping down the rest of the candy bar as I went. I greeted my arriving students and waved them on into the agility field as I passed and tried to direct Buck to park his car beside the house and out of the way of new arrivals. Like a typical male, he ignored my gesticulations and pulled up right in front of the training building, blocking the entrance.

"Oh, for heaven's sake, Buck," I began as he got out of the car, "can't you see we're having class here? I've got another dozen people due in the next fifteen minutes and you're in the way."

I noticed the grim set to Buck's mouth about the same time the passenger door opened and another man got out. He was not anyone I knew, about forty, I guessed, and not very distinguished looking—dark haired, light skinned, and, in the middle of the summer heat, wearing a suit.

Buck said, "Raine, this is Special Agent Tom Dickerson, from the FBI."

My jaw dropped. I stared stupidly and said, "The FB- *what?*"

I'm really not that unsophisticated, and I've been around law enforcement for a while, but I couldn't help being taken aback. Generally the only federal agents we see around here are on television. What was Buck doing riding around with one in his car?

I felt heat creeping up my cheeks at the clumsiness of my welcome, but before I could extricate myself I had bigger problems. A golden blur crossed my peripheral vision just as I saw a look of dismay on Buck's face. Apparently one of the students had left the gate open to the agility field. Cisco launched himself into the air and onto Buck's chest about half a second before I cried, "Damn it, Cisco, don't!"

Cisco is wild about Buck and can never greet him in a normally demonstrative way. Worse, Buck continues to reinforce his bad behavior. Even on duty, even in a freshly pressed uniform and even in front of the FBI, for heaven's sake, Buck took a moment to scratch the grinning golden retriever's ears and say gently, "Hi there, big fella."

Satisfied, Cisco flung himself away from Buck and, before I could catch his collar, spun toward the visitor. I'm quite sure Cisco didn't have time to do any more than brush up against the neat dark material of the man's government suit before I shouted, "Cisco, here!" in a way that brooked no argument. My big, happy, clumsy oaf bounced over to me and did a perfect sit-in-front, gazing up at me in grinning anticipation of his treat while Mr. FBI Agent brushed imaginary paw prints from his clothes.

Not, apparently, a dog lover. He fell a notch in my esteem.

I fished a liver treat out of my pocket and tossed it to Cisco. He caught it expertly, midair. I said, "Cisco, go lie down."

"Go lie down" is a great command. It gives the dog freedom to choose his place and doesn't bind him to any particular position, but it gets him out of your way. It also has the rather useful side effect of making it look as though your dog understands conversational English, when all he really has to know are two words: "go," which means to move away from the person who said it, and "down," which every puppy who's been through one of my classes knows.

Like the obedience champion he would never be, Cisco got up, walked purposefully toward a patch of shade on the dusty ground, and dropped down on his side, panting and watching us expectantly.

Mr. Dickerson did not appear to be impressed. He had stopped brushing at his clothes and was staring at me like—well, like I had chocolate on my face. I actually brushed my hand across my mouth to make sure, and then I realized he was reading my hat. I didn't think a guy like him would get the joke even if I explained it, so I didn't bother. Besides, by now I was so flustered I wasn't entirely sure even I could remember what was supposed to be funny about having "I Run Naked" embroidered on a hat.

"Mr. Dickerson," I said in a take-charge way I was far from feeling, "I'm Raine Stockton." I stuck out my hand, remembered the hot dogs and liver treats, wiped my hand on my shorts and offered it again. "It's nice to meet you." He shook my hand with only a minimal show of reluctance, and he did get points for not wiping it with his handkerchief when he was through. Well, what did he expect, for heaven's sake? I train dogs.

Buck said, "Raine, this isn't a social visit. Can we go inside and talk?"

I didn't like the way he sounded, all pompous and official, and at first I thought he was just showing off for the FBI. But then I noted the grimness in his eyes, and I *really* didn't like that. In fact, when a policeman says, "This is not a social visit," I can't imagine anyone in her right mind who could find anything to like about the whole situation.

I said, stupidly, "Is anything wrong?"

Buck jerked his head toward the door, and I didn't feel I had any choice but to lead them inside. First, however, I walked over and snapped a leash on Cisco—during training class I always keep one draped around my neck like a stole— and brought him around the side of the building to an outdoor enclosed run, where I left him to play with my two Aussies, Mischief and Magic. I tried to look cheerful and confident for all the students who were giving me curious, concerned looks as I led the two lawmen into the office and closed the door. Then I didn't bother to look cheerful at all.

My heart beating hard, I said, "Is it Uncle Roe? Has something happened to him?"

That was honestly the only thing I could think of that would cause this kind of commotion and the grim look on Buck's face. My uncle Roe was the sheriff of Hanover County and had been for most of my life. The part of my brain that remembered anything at all about the law knew logically that if there had been an accusation of malfeasance in the sheriff's office, the state would be investigating, not the federal government, and if something worse had happened to my uncle in the line of duty, Buck would not bring the FBI with him to break the news to me. But it was really all I could think of.

The two men stood awkwardly in the small room, which was already overcrowded with a desk, file cabinet and coffeemaker. There was a corner table piled high with brochures—house-training your dog, nutrition for the growing puppy, the importance of dental care—that we got free from the pet food companies, and underneath it were several thirty-pound bags of dog food.

The bulletin board was crammed with photos of students and former students, some of them proudly sporting ribbons, and randomly decorated with announcements of upcoming events. In one corner was a standing rack of various-sized collars and leashes, which we sell to those students who come to us without knowing what size their dogs should wear, along with a few clip-on treat bags and head harnesses. On the floor beside it was a plastic bag filled with five hundred logo-printed clickers, which we give away.

There was a battered old refrigerator in which we kept soft drinks, hot dogs, and medication for the boarders when their owners brought it in, as well as whatever special food needed refrigeration. Glancing around, I was glad I had taken the time to straighten up this weekend.

There was a sagging sofa covered with dog hair—as well it should be, since most of those who sat on it were dogs—and I gestured them to it impatiently. My throat grew drier by the minute. I sat on the molded plastic dog crate that served as a coffee table and leaned forward urgently. "What's wrong? Has something happened?"

Tom Dickerson reached into his coat pocket and brought out a photo. "Miss Stockton, do you know this man?"

I looked at the photo and my heart stopped pounding. It stopped beating at all for what seemed like a very long time.

I looked at Buck. His face was a mask. I made mine the same, but I didn't have to work very hard at it. I was so stunned, so shaken by the flood of memories and emotions, that I didn't know what to feel first, so I felt, and thought, nothing at all.

In a voice so calm I hardly recognized it, I said, "That's Andy Fontana. Of course I know him. Everyone knows him."

Dickerson said, "But you know him better than most, don't you?"

"I don't know what you mean by that."

I really didn't. What did he mean, "You *know* him better than most"? I hadn't seen Andy in fifteen years. I had thought about him even less, and when I did I assumed, like most other people, that he was dead.

"Didn't you date him in college?"

I cut a sharp glance toward Buck. He said nothing. Why wasn't he saying anything?

All of a sudden I began to understand that this was serious. Very serious. I felt my shoulders square, as though for battle, as I leaned my weight back on my hands.

"I dated Andy in high school once or twice," I replied. "I lived with him in college."

No point in lying about it. He wouldn't have asked the question had he not already known the answer. And there were no secrets from Buck about my past with Andy. Well, not many.

"When was the last time you heard from him?"

Now *that* surprised me. "What do you mean, the last time? Gosh, I don't know. Not since college. I don't remember. You people asked me all these questions before, when Andy was under investigation."

"Not since then?"

"No, of course not, not since then. No one has heard from him since then, at least not that I know of." Agent Dickerson tucked the photo back into his pocket. I looked at Buck in confusion.

Buck said, "Andy is back is the country, Raine. We think he might be headed this way."

Chapter Four

About a dozen thoughts went through my head, and all of them at once. I wondered how they knew. I wondered how Andy had managed it. I wondered how and why and if, and all the while my heart was pounding about two beats ahead of my brain. Andy was alive. He was headed this way.

I said, looking straight at the FBI agent without blinking, "If he makes it to these mountains, you're screwed."

Possibly that wasn't the brightest thing to say, even though it was exactly what I was thinking. I could feel Buck's hard look and imagined that if we'd been alone he would have slapped at me with the back of his hat, one of his favorite ways of getting my attention when he thought I was close to going too far—or had already done it.

A quirk of the federal agent's lips suggested I might have been too hasty in assuming he had no sense of humor. He said, "We're aware of that, Miss Stockton." Andy, like most of the boys—and some of the girls—around here, had spent his youth roaming the woods and the hills, fishing, hunting, camping, exploring. That's what kids did, and you weren't a man in this part of the world until your daddy handed you your first .22 rifle and took you out into the woods to kill something.

But for Andy the mountains were more than a place to spend a Saturday, more even than a rite of passage. To him they were almost sacred. I used to tease him that I thought he'd live there like a caveman if he wasn't afraid the truant officers would get him, and then he'd always toss back, "They'd have to find me first!"

There was as much truth in that now as then. No one knew these mountains better than Andy Fontana.

Well, almost no one.

I said, "Is there some reason you think he's coming here? I mean, he's got to know this is the first place you're going to look."

But apparently this was not the federal government's day for answering questions. Agent Dickerson said, "If he does make it this far, we think it's possible that he might try to contact you."

I frowned. "I don't know why you'd think that. I suspect it's the last thing he'd do."

For the first time, Dickerson looked interested. "Oh? Why's that?"

"For one thing, we didn't exactly part on the best of terms. I broke up with him and married a cop. For another, it's been fifteen years. He's got plenty of other people he would go to long before he'd call on an old girlfriend who he last accused of being a patsy for the right-wing establishment that was plotting to kill this planet."

After a moment, Dickerson nodded and took a business card from his pocket. "Nonetheless, you'll let us know if he does try to contact you."

Not a question but a statement. And how stupid would I have been to say no? I took the card, glanced at it and noticed it contained a local number. A cell phone? Or had they set up a task force in town already? Were they *that* sure Andy was headed here?

And all this before word of his return had even made the local newscast.

I placed the card carefully on the desk and stood as they did. I walked with them to the door and into the corridor, where the sound of barking dogs echoed from the training room, the boarding kennels and the outdoor runs.

"That big golden of yours," Dickerson commented, obviously trying to make friends now that business was over. "Nice dog. Do you ever hunt with him?"

"Sometimes." I opened the door to the outside sunshine and let them pass through first. "In a way. We hunt people mostly. Search and rescue."

I doubt this came as any surprise to him. After all, even if he hadn't pulled up every scrap of information ever collected on me, both public and private, before the interview, what else would he and Buck have talked about on the way over?

It seemed as though we had been in the office forever, but in fact less than ten minutes had passed. People were still driving up, unloading dogs, greeting one another. Dickerson turned to me. "It was a pleasure meeting you, Miss Stockton." He shook my hand. "I know we can count on your cooperation."

There was something vaguely intimidating about that, but I shook his hand anyway. Buck just stood there beside the open car door, silent and expressionless.

"Hi, Raine!"

Sonny Brightwell was getting out of her van with her border collie, Mystery, clinging to her leg like a burr. She started over to us. "Hi, Buck. How's it going?"

Buck nodded to her and touched his hat, then got into the car without a word.

Sonny reached me just as Buck was making the three-point turn that would lead him back out the drive. "What's the matter with him?" she asked, eyebrow raised.

After a moment I shrugged. I would have liked a straight answer to that myself. "Oh, he's just playing big-time cop for the guy in the suit."

I leaned down and scratched Mystery's chin. "How's my pretty girl?"

Mystery had adopted Sonny only a few months ago, but already the two were inseparable. Since then, Sonny had been through two rounds of obedience classes with the border collie, had a herding instructor come to her house twice a week and had now decided that Mystery was ready to learn agility. Sonny is exactly the kind of owner every dog deserves and few of them get, and I was enormously proud of the small role I had played in bringing the two of them together.

Sonny regaled me with an account of Mystery's latest adventures as we walked toward the agility field. "She's making a lot of progress since I explained to her that the point of herding sheep is not to chase them until they fall down, but to keep them all together and move them toward the pen. She thought all I wanted was to tire the sheep out, and I have to admit, she does have a point—the sheep are a lot easier to handle when they're exhausted."

Talking to Sonny about dogs always makes for an interesting conversation, since she never fails to include the dogs' opinions on the matter. The thing is, Sonny Brightwell, a highly accomplished and extremely successful lawyer from the coastal regions, claims she can communicate with animals—and not like I communicate with them, with a treat and a happy word of praise, but really *talk* to them, and hear them talking back. And though the entire concept is complete nonsense, there are times when I think I almost believe her.

When Cisco and Mystery ran away into the woods in March, I'm not sure we would have ever found either of them if it hadn't been for Sonny's insight into Mystery's thought processes. And if I were to be completely honest, I probably owed her more than I had ever admitted for the rescue of Angel Winston, the little girl who disappeared during that same episode. What Sonny had relayed to me about Cisco's unique perspective on the situation had led me to the evidence that eventually solved the mystery of where she was and brought Angel home safely.

Since that time Sonny and I had become better friends than anyone might have predicted, given the fact that we have so little in common. She was ten, maybe fifteen years older than I was, tall and statuesque. She wore her long gray hair in a thick braid and dressed in peasant skirts and colorful shawls when she wasn't training her dog. She was an avid idealist and, as previously indicated, a bit of a flake in some respects. She was also extremely wealthy and by all accounts one of the sharpest lawyers to ever practice in this state.

By contrast I was dull, pragmatic and ordinary, and the two of us agreed on only two things: our dogs and our love of these mountains. Still, I enjoyed her company and usually looked forward to her visits. Today, however, I was a little too distracted to give my full attention to Sonny's stories.

"Well, you need to be careful," I commented absently. "An exhausted sheep can fall down dead in this heat." She gave me a quick, odd look and changed the subject. "Will Cisco be coming to class today? Mystery has been looking forward to seeing him."

Sometimes I took advantage of the class situation to proof-train my own dogs by using them to demonstrate the correct behaviors, and up until this spring, Cisco had been my primary agility dog. But Cisco had issues: He was afraid of the dog walk, he was slow on the A-frame and he didn't like to run so far ahead of me that he couldn't see me. Since I was still officially supposed to be recovering from knee surgery, I wasn't as fast as I once had been, and the whole situation was just too frustrating.

So after three disappointing competitions in a row, I had temporarily taken Cisco out of agility and put him into obedience training. There's only so much humiliation a person can take, after all, and it was a lot more fun to train a dog who actually had a chance at winning—like an Australian shepherd.

I answered, "I don't think so."

"Maybe they can play after class."

"Sure."

Sonny gave me another odd look and I wondered whether she could read people's minds as well as animals'. But all she said was, "I'll see you over there, then," and she took Mystery off to the exercise area—a euphemism for the canine latrine, where the students gathered with their dogs before class.

I called the class to order and explained the exercises for the day, and within minutes the disturbing episode with Buck and the FBI receded to the back of my mind. I really do love working with dogs, whether they're my own or someone else's, and agility class is the most fun because everyone is there just to have fun with the dogs.

I supervised the handlers as one by one they guided their dogs over the three low jumps and through the tunnel. When it came time to add the A-frame to the sequence, I asked whether I could borrow Mystery to demonstrate. As a general rule, few dogs can outshine a border collie in agility, although I liked to think I had a couple of Australian shepherds who might, and Mystery usually worked for me as well as she did for Sonny. But there was another reason I asked to borrow Mystery.

Though few people would believe it to see her now, a mere three months ago Sonny had been in a wheelchair. Though she has improved a hundred, maybe even a thousand, percent since the active little border collie came into her life, she suffers from a crippling form of rheumatoid arthritis that is only partially controlled by

40

medication. Midway through agility class she is always exhausted but refuses to rest for fear of depriving her dog of class time. So I usually find a way to take over for her.

And by the time I had taken Mystery through the sequence twice, I could barely even remember the FBI agent's name.

"She really has potential," I told Sonny at the end of class, blotting my sweaty face with the sleeve of my T-shirt. I waved good-bye to another student and her very promising young Labrador retriever and felt obligated to add, "Of course, a lot of these dogs do."

Sonny gathered up her supplies—dog treats, bottled water, squeaky toys—and stuffed them into her carrying bag. "She enjoys it," she told me. "She says she can beat any dog in class."

I had to chuckle at that. "She probably could. Why don't you bring her to the dog show this weekend? It would do her good to be around all the noise and excitement, especially if she's ever going to compete."

Sonny smiled and shook her head. "I don't think we're up for competition."

"There are going to be tons of vendors there, selling all kinds of cool dog stuff."

"Well, now you're talking." Sonny rose from the bench where handlers and dogs rested between turns and tried to disguise her grimace with a smile. "Maybe we could drive up and watch you compete. What time do you start?"

"On Saturday I'm taking Cisco through novice obedience at eight, and Mischief should be running agility around noon. Maude is showing heir male golden in utility—that's advanced obedience—and that should be something to see."

"No sheep?"

"No sheep."

"We can probably be there in time to watch you run Mischief. Sounds like fun."

"And lots of shopping." I added, "Do you want to put the dogs in the play yard for a while?"

As we walked toward the kennels and the side play yard that opened off them, she said, "I guess you heard about the court decision." Mystery scampered back and forth, barking for us to hurry up, and Cisco, hearing the excitement in her voice, responded in kind from the kennels.

"What?" There was no point in shouting at the dogs to be quiet; besides, I was accustomed to talking over the sound of barking. "No. What decision?"

"Oh." She looked surprised. "You seemed distracted when I came in. I just assumed you'd heard. Our petition for a hearing was denied."

It took me a moment to switch gears and register what it was she was talking about. It's not that the issue wasn't important to me; it was in fact of monumental importance. It was just that there had been a couple of things on my mind today that were of slightly more immediate importance, and only one of them was agility class.

I should explain that in addition to being a semi-retired attorney and an excellent dog owner, Sonny was currently spearheading an opposition movement against the development company that planned to turn our little corner of paradise into a fly-in golf resort for the superrich and the companies they owned.

She had helped to form a resistance group called Save the Mountains and had talked me into serving on the board. She thought my expertise in wildlife management and the environment would be useful, and that my status as a "native" would engage the sympathies of the public—not to mention that the mountain for which this development was being planned was literally in my own backyard.

Sonny had filed a petition for a hearing to determine the legality of proceeding with the project before we, the Save the Mountains group, had an opportunity to complete our own environmental impact study. She had explained at the time that our likelihood of success with the petition was slim, but it was the first in a series of necessary steps.

If my father had still been sitting on the bench, our request would have been granted without a second thought. But I guess things were done a little differently these days.

Currently, my view was of blue-, green- and purple-shadowed wilderness, relieved only by the occasional glint of a pink-white rhododendron blossom peering from the shadows. But if the proposed project could not be stopped, it was only a matter of time before my side of the mountain was scarred by earth movers just like Valley Street was.

Needless to say, I was *not* a huge fan of the development project. And although I generally tried to avoid politics, my opposition put me squarely on the side of the "troublemakers," as the Save the Mountains group was already being called in some circles.

I said, "No. I didn't hear. Are we going to appeal?"

"We have several options, and that's one of them. I'm going to draft an e-mail for the board tonight."

We let Mystery into the play yard and I reached over the fence to unlock the gate of Cisco's kennel. He came barreling out like a racehorse, tripped over his own fast-moving feet and Mystery's even faster-moving ones, rolled three times and came up galloping with Mystery nipping at his flying tail. I had to grin at their antics. Mystery was much faster than Cisco, but she liked to catch his tail feathering in her mouth, so she always played chase. When Cisco got tired of that he would spin and start chasing her, and off she would go like a bullet. He never caught on that he didn't have a prayer of catching her.

What I had forgotten, of course, was that Magic and Mischief were in the same pen as Cisco. About two seconds after Cisco shot into the yard, they both came tumbling out. I managed to snag Magic's collar and turn her back into the pen, but Mischief was like a bolt of lightning. She was halfway across the yard before I even knew she was gone.

Mischief was thirty-five pounds of pure energy. When she wasn't actually getting into trouble, she was thinking about getting into trouble, which is of course how she got her name. She and Magic had come into my canine family a little over a year before, when a passerby had found the two of them happily playing in the tall grass by the highway and had taken them to our local vet for safekeeping. The vet called me, and I agreed to foster the pups until I could find them a good home. It took me about three weeks to realize they had already found a good home—mine.

As impossible as it seems, people do actually abandon purebred dogs, and that appeared to be what had happened to Mischief and Magic. They were almost perfect representatives of the Australian shepherd breed. Each had that gorgeous blue merle coloring that is typical of the breed—a kind of swirled-up mixture of gray and black that gives the coat a silvery blue cast—offset by brilliant white collars. Their eyes were gemstone blue, and their tails had been docked, which is customary for the breed. Mischief had a white patch over her left eye, and Magic had a black mask outlining her face. Otherwise they were almost identical in appearance, although Mischief's energy level and jumping ability made her easy to distinguish from Magic.

Australian shepherds are, as the name implies, herding dogs, although they actually are an American breed, not an Australian one. They are known for their speed, their quick intelligence and their agility, as well as their natural herding ability. Because their compact build enables them to make quick turns and fast starts and stops, they excel in sports such as agility. I had big plans for Mischief on the agility course—if I could just get her to focus on learning the obstacles instead of running wildly around looking for trouble.

Generally I don't like to turn more than two dogs out at a time, and three is an especially bad number. Pack behavior often causes two of the dogs to gang up on another, and although that makes an interesting social study to watch, I didn't have room for it in my kennel.

But I quickly saw that I had nothing to worry about. Mischief, who could leap over my head from a standing start and who had been known to jump on the kitchen table, snatch up my lunch and make off with it before all four paws even grazed the tabletop, sailed over Cisco's back, executed a perfect pivot in mid-flight, and began chasing *him*. Mystery naturally took exception to that, since up until that point the game had been hers. She tore after Mischief, barking an angry challenge, and poor Cisco knew he was outclassed. One lap around the yard and he flung <u>him</u>self on the grass, panting hard, and left the chase to the girls.

"Holy cow, she's fast," observed Sonny, laughing a little as Mischief, outfoxing Mystery, leapt over the supine Cisco, did a one-eighty and took off in the opposite direction.

"Yeah," I agreed proudly. "She is."

Sonny chuckled. "Cisco says he could outrun both of them if he wanted to."

"Yeah, he looks like he could," I observed dryly as my exhausted dog rolled in the grass.

"He says he only lets Mystery win because she likes it. He's much faster than she is."

"Spoken like a true male." This came from Maude, who had come up beside us without my noticing. Of course, with all the ruckus from the kennel it would be hard to notice a 747 landing in the yard.

I smiled and so did Sonny, and I had to call Mischief only three times to get her to come over to me. When she did, I gave her a treat and a big hug and happily escorted her back to her kennel.

When I returned, Sonny was explaining to Maude about the denied petition. I didn't catch all the legalities and I wasn't much interested in them. One of the leftover rebellions from my childhood was a stubborn determination not to understand anything a lawyer said. But I gathered the bottom line was that we had to take a different approach.

"The first thing we have to do," Sonny was saying, "is to show we're making a good-faith effort to *start* an environmental impact study. That means bringing in experts from UNC and North Carolina State University, or even from Washington, D.C., if we have to."

"Sounds expensive," Maude said.

"These things usually are."

"Well, I can save you some money," I said. "You want to know about the environmental impact of tearing up the mountain? Just ask Caralee Tucker over on Valley Street. She had a five-hundred-pound bear in her workshop this morning."

Sonny's eyes widened. She hadn't lived here long enough to know that bears in the summer were about as common as hummingbirds—although perhaps not quite as welcome. "Five hundred pounds? Are you kidding?"

I shrugged. "Well, probably not five hundred pounds. Bears always look a little bigger indoors than out. But you don't have to search much farther than that if you want to see a *real* environmental impact."

Sonny sighed. "Well, I hope I won't sound like too much of a flatlander if I say I'd rather read about it in a well-constructed report than confront it in my workshop, or anywhere else for that matter."

She smiled as Mystery, who had completed the mandatory border collie circuit of the play yard, sniffing every blade of grass upon which Mischief had put her paws, finally flopped down beside Cisco, panting as heavily as he was. "Well, I know one little black-and-white dog who will be sleeping well tonight."

"I think they've both had their exercise for the day," I agreed.

I opened the gate and called the dogs over. They came with tongues lolling and tails wagging but with a noticeably lesser <u>amo</u>unt of energy. Sonny snapped a leash on Mystery and I patted my chest, inviting Cisco up for a back rub.

"See you next week," Sonny said.

Cisco placed his paws on my chest and I ruffled his fur. "I'll probably talk to you before then. Meantime, work on Mystery's start-line stay this week. She's got to learn to wait until you give the command before she takes the first obstacle."

Sonny nodded and waved to us both as she walked Mystery back to her van.

"And now," said Maude, giving Cisco a brisk pat as she turned to me, "perhaps you would be good enough to tell me what interest the Federal Bureau of Investigation has in you?"

Chapter Five

I had forgotten about the agent's business card, which I had left on the desk. I should have made a point to tell Maude about the visit before class, since I'm sure she had noticed the patrol car blocking our customer parking area, and the stranger who had accompanied Buck into the closed-door meeting with me in the office.

I sighed. "Come on. I'll tell you about it while we clean up." And I gave her as detailed a description of the interview as I could.

"So," was Maude's only comment when the tale was told, "Andy is back in town."

"Not necessarily," I pointed out quickly. "Not necessarily even headed here. That's just the theory." "Perhaps." She handed me a broom and took one for herself, and we started at opposite ends of the training room, sweeping dog hair and scattered treats toward the center. "But one would think a government agency as experienced as the FBI would have just cause before forming a theory like that."

"I suppose."

"I always thought you should have married him, you know."

That got my attention. I stopped mid-sweep. "Andy?"

"Oh, absolutely. You two always had so much more in common than you and Buck. Hooligans to the core, both of you." She chuckled. "Do you remember that time you stole your father's automobile?"

I resumed sweeping. "We didn't steal it; we borrowed it."

"You 'borrowed' it halfway to the Tennessee border," she retorted. "And when it broke down on the highway, who did you call to come pick you up?"

I grinned. "I'm not sure I ever thanked you for that, Maude."

"Fortunately, it was only the fan belt. Anything more complex and we would have had to call a tow truck." Among Maude's many other talents, she was an excellent mechanic. She told me it was a skill she had picked up while serving in the Royal Air Force. However she had acquired her familiarity with fan belts and other moving parts of the internal combustion engine, on the night in question it was a godsend. We had had my father's car back in the garage before sunup, and his daughter back in her bed, and neither he nor my mother had ever been aware that either one of them had gone missing.

Of course, Maude had assured us that if questioned directly, she would not lie for us. But we managed our adventure so excellently that there was no reason for anyone to ever be questioned about anything.

Maude said, "Where did you think you were

going in Tennessee, anyway? I'm not sure I ever knew."

I grinned as I swept my pile of dog hair to meet hers, then bent to rake both piles into an oversized covered dustpan. "The Chattanooga Choo Choo."

"The what?"

"You know. Like the song. It's a tourist thing. We just decided we wanted to see it."

"You would have never gotten away with it."

I glanced at her askance. "Wanna bet?"

"Actually, no. I dread to think what you did manage to get away with that none of us knew about."

Maude was polite enough not to mention the things we had not gotten away with that almost everyone knew about: a little petty shoplifting, carrying less than an ounce of a controlled substance—this was back in the day when that was still a misdemeanor and jail time was not mandatory—underage drinking, trespassing, breaking curfew and minor property damage. All of these charges sound so much worse than they were—except maybe the drugs and the underage drinking—and we always had a good reason.

We broke a car window because a dog had been left inside in ninety-degree heat. We were caught trespassing inside the high school records office after hours because Andy believed that a particular teacher had illegally raised an athlete's letter grade so that he could continue to play. He was, of course, right. We shoplifted cigarettes because Andy wanted to prove how stupid the laws against selling cigarettes to minors were...but unfortunately, it turned out on that occasion that he was wrong.

Andy always had a dragon to slay, a case to prove. And because I was a romantic teenager who, by way of a side benefit, wanted to prove that her parents' values were not necessarily her own, I was always right by his side with guns blazing.

"At least it was the Choo Choo," I pointed out, "which some people might even have called educational, instead of a rock concert."

"Precisely. And I suppose that's one reason I always liked the boy. He was unusual like that. Now, if it had been Buck you had chosen to go joyriding with, it would have been to a rock concert."

I had never thought about it that way before, but she was probably right. Odd, the way things turn out. The way people turn out.

"Of course," Maude added, "all of that only goes to show how wrong a person can be." She emptied the dustpan into a plastic-bag-lined trashcan and twisted the bag closed. "What did Buck have to say about the news?"

I made a dry face. "Buck did not take the opportunity to express his opinions to me."

"Which should not by any means suggest he doesn't have them."

"Oh, he has opinions, all right." I gave the training room a cursory sweep with my eyes before deciding it would do until our twice-weekly deep cleaning on Saturday afternoon. "And I can't wait to hear what they are."

As it happened, I did not have to wait long. At five o'clock, just as I was doling out super-premium kibble into three waiting bowls (Cisco, who is on a hypoallergenic diet, gets homemade food), the phone rang. I was actually surprised to hear Buck's voice, because anyone who knows me knows I feed the dogs at five o'clock, and that it is not a good time to call. They were lined up like life-sized statues, Cisco on one end and Majesty, the rough collie, on the other, with the two Australian shepherds in the middle; four pairs of eyes were fixed on me with rapt expectation, and long strings of anticipatory drool dripped from at least two sets of jowls. As long as the promise of dinner was mere moments away, they would remain like that, fixed and attentive, pretending to be the kind of perfectly behaved animals that actually earned their super-premium kibble. But the minute I turned my attention away from the preparation of their meal, I would lose my tenuous measure of control, and a riot would ensue.

So before answering the phone I held up my hand in the classic "stay" gesture and made a point to tuck Cisco's empty bowl under my arm before answering the phone. The rule around here was that no one ate until everyone was served, and they knew that as long as I still had one bowl to fill, there was hope. I answered the phone and opened the refrigerator door at the same time. "Hey," Buck said. "You want to grab a burger?"

"I'm feeding the dogs."

"I mean afterward."

"You're on duty." I took out the big plastic bowl of chopped chicken hearts and oatmeal and set it on the counter.

"I get a dinner break. How about seven?"

"Did your buddy at the agency go home?" I

found a spoon and shoveled a measure of glop into Cisco's bowl. Watching me, he licked his lips and shifted his paws but did not move.

"Come on, Raine." He sounded a little uncomfortable. "He's a nice enough guy. So how about dinner?"

I put the lid back on the plastic bowl and returned it to the refrigerator. One by one I put the bowls on the floor, about six feet apart, and shifted the receiver away from my mouth. "Release," I said to the dogs, and in a perfect symphony of movement they charged to their individual bowls and began chowing down.

"I don't know," I said to Buck, "I'm tired. I've still got all the kennel dogs to feed and exercise. I don't want to go back out."

"Okay, then. I'll give Effie your best."

Effie, of Effie's Route 2 Diner, served the best french fries this side of France. This side of anywhere. Rumor had it that people traveled four states out of their way for Effie's french fries, and if I had had to, I would have been one of them.

I said, "Seven thirty. I still have to shower."

"See you there."

We have room for twenty-five boarders, and between the first of June and the last of August we are almost always full. This is good for the business, since more than half the year's income is earned in those two months, and bad for the employees—namely Maude and me—because twenty-five dogs are a lot of dogs to keep fed, watered, cleaned and exercised.

Generally we feed between five thirty and six, turn the dogs out in pairs into the play yard for one last run, and try to have everyone bedded down by eight. Usually Maude goes home after the dishes are cleaned from the five thirty feeding, and I don't mind taking the last exercise duty, cleaning the yard of poop and making sure all the dogs are comfortably tucked in before lights-out.

On the rare occasion when I go out at night, or she does, it's easy enough to condense the process. We divided the kennel in half; I took the big dogs and she took the small, and everyone was fed, watered, cleaned and exercised by seven.

Fortunately, my short curly brown hair actually looks better wet than dry, so I just toweled it dry after my shower. I slipped into a yellow skort and striped top, which was dressy enough for Effie's, and applied a quick brush of lip gloss. I was on the road by seven fifteen.

The restaurant wasn't as crowded on a Wednesday night as it would be on the weekend, but I saw plenty of people I knew. I waved to a couple of neighbors and stopped to say hello to the Baptist preacher, and when Effie saw me she said, "He's in the back, Raine. How y'all doing tonight?"

"Good, thanks. Did Buck order me a burger?"

"Medium well with a stack of fries," she replied, waving over her shoulder as she passed. "It'll be up in about fifteen minutes. Sweet tea is on the table."

"Thanks, Effie." I made my way to the back room. Effie's had been one of the last eateries to go smoke free, and up until a year ago the back room had been the smoking area. It held only about six tables, and tonight only one of them was occupied. I thought I knew why Buck had wanted a table where we wouldn't be seen, or heard, and it annoyed me. By tomorrow morning someone would have told someone else that they had seen my almost-ex-husband and me cozied up together in the back room at Effie's, and by the end of the week people would be stopping me on the street to ask when Buck was moving back in.

So I greeted him with, "This is dumb. There are plenty of tables out front."

He said, "I ordered your burger."

I slid into the booth opposite him, my thighs sticking a little on the vinyl. "Where's Wyn? I thought she was going to be with you."

Wyn was Buck's partner on the force and possibly the only woman in Hanover County he had not slept with. In a way it was too bad because she was also one of the few women I knew who could have whipped him into shape. But spending twelve hours a day in a patrol car with him had apparently neutralized whatever attraction might have developed, because she couldn't have been less interested.

Buck answered, "You know she's on vacation."

"Oh. I forgot."

I picked up the tall amber glass of iced tea and twisted around in my seat to look for Effie. "I need a straw. I hate sitting back here. You can't see anything, and they always forget about you."

Buck rolled a paper-covered straw across the table to me. He said, "I wanted to talk to you about this afternoon."

"You acted like a jerk."

"I know." He leaned back and propped one elbow on the back of the booth, pushing his fingers through his hair. His lips were tight at the corners, and he looked disgusted with himself.

"I didn't mean to spring it on you," he said. "But, damn it, they had just sprung it on me about an hour earlier. What a thing to happen, huh? Roe has pulled in every man for full-time duty and canceled all time off until further notice. Good thing Wyn is on that cruise or she'd be dragged back too."

"I don't see why." I stripped the paper covering off my straw and plopped it into the tea glass. "There's no sign that Andy's in this area, right? Or really even headed here. That's just the FBI's theory. Right?"

Buck did not answer. In fact, he didn't meet my eyes.

I repeated, pausing with the straw almost to my lips, "Right?"

Buck blew out a breath and looked at me. "Oh, hell," he said. "You'll find out soon enough anyway. Apparently he's been back in the country for some time. He's been in touch with people."

I put the tea down un-tasted. "Somebody turned him in?" Buck held my gaze steadily. "The FBI tends to keep a close watch on the known associates of the people on their most-wanted list. Nobody had to turn him in."

I got the message, and I resented it. "I don't suppose you happened to mention that you used to be one of Andy's known associates?"

He scowled. "I told the FBI everything I know about Andy Fontana."

"Including the fact that, up until you stole his girl, he was your best friend?"

Silence. Buck didn't blink, and neither did I.

Then Buck said quietly, "Funny. The way I remember it, Andy stole his best friend's girl."

No one overhearing the conversation or reading our tight, hostile body language would believe it, but up until then things had been going really well between Buck and me. And I liked it when things went well.

I liked it when he called me after he got off shift in the morning and I would take a few minutes to stretch out on the sofa with a cup of coffee, knowing that he was stretched out on the sofa with a cup of coffee in his house. and we just talked. I liked it when he dropped by to play a game of ball with the dogs or brought me lunch for no reason, and I liked calling him up when I wanted to go to a movie or to a show out of town. I liked looking up in the bleachers when I had a dog show and seeing him there, cheering me on, just like old times.

The fact of the matter is, when all is said and done, it's a lot nicer to get along with your ex than to have him for an enemy. And most of the time I liked Buck; I really did. I was even starting to think I might be able to put aside the multiple infidelities that had been the real cause of our broken marriage and learn to trust him again. But now all of a sudden here we were stabbing and slicing at each other like the pros we were. That was what Andy Fontana had always done to us.

I was the first to lower my gaze, and I took a sip of tea. I said, "I guess we both betrayed Andy, didn't we?"

Buck said sharply, "He's the one who did the betraying, Raine. Of our trust, of the law, of everything this country stands for. I think you need to remember that."

"Would that be the same country where a man

is innocent until proven guilty?" I shot back. "Thank you, Mr. High and Mighty Upholder of the Law!"

"Damn it, Raine, would you just tell me what makes you so sure Andy was innocent—despite everything the best-trained law enforcement officers in the country believed to the contrary?"

I leaned across the table toward him. "Because I never heard one shred of hard evidence against him. Because I knew Andy. There wasn't a violent bone in his body. And because, unlike some people, I'm loyal to my friends."

Buck glared at me. "Maybe you didn't know Andy as well as you think. And this has got nothing to do with loyalty."

"Nobody was ever able to prove that he was even in the area when that building was bombed. And what did Andy know about bombs, anyway? He was a dreamer, a poet, a naturalist. His weapons were words, not explosives!"

Buck drew in a sharp breath through his nostrils and I saw frustration flare in his eyes. Because I knew him so well I could see his last-minute decision to bite back words he knew he would later regret. What he said instead was, "I've been hunting with Andy, and let me tell you, he knew plenty about weapons."

"Yeah, well, you show me the squirrel he bombed out of a tree and we'll have something to talk about." I scowled and looked impatiently over my shoulder. "Where's my hamburger?"

Buck picked up his glass, looked at it and set it down again. "Raine, listen. This is serious stuff, okay? And it could get a lot more serious."

I looked at him, and I saw the kind of deep,

troubled expression in his eyes that I hadn't seen since…well, since Andy had been the object of a manhunt all those years ago. Back then I had thought it was because of all the personal anguish the situation had brought into our lives—the questions, the notoriety and the very real possibility that Buck's career in law enforcement, then only in its infancy, would be damaged forever by association. Not to mention how adversely his young marriage was being affected by the problems of his wife's old lover. And now he had even more to lose.

Except, of course, he had already lost me.

He went on, "It's so serious that I could get into big trouble for even talking to you about this. So I'm counting on you to keep things to yourself, okay?"

I shrugged uncomfortably. "There's nothing to keep. There's nobody to tell. This is a non-issue."

"Good. Because the FBI is trying to keep this whole investigation under wraps for now. The last thing we need is a caravan of news trucks parked in front of the courthouse like we had in March."

He was referring to the Angel Winston case, which had made news around the southeast when the little girl went missing in the frozen wilderness.

I said, "Well, good luck with that. This is a small town and Andy is a hometown boy. It won't take long for word to get out. And by the way, if discretion is what the FBI has in mind, they did a pretty poor job of it this afternoon. I mean, that Agent Dickerson might as well have been wearing a sign over his head."

"People can talk all they want, as long as they

don't know what's really going on."

"Spoken like a genuine defender of truth, justice and the American way."

The aroma of grilled beef, steamed onions and golden French fries wafted into the room a good three seconds before Effie herself appeared bearing two heaping platters. My mouth watered, and all the unpleasantness of the previous conversation completely evaporated with the promise of the feast. After all, I hadn't had anything to eat all day except a bag of peanuts and a Snickers bar.

Effie set the plates before us, snagged a bottle of ketchup from a nearby table and said, "Y'all gonna be okay? Anything else?"

"Thanks, Effie; this is great." I stacked bun, lettuce and tomato atop the fat burger. "Another napkin when you get the chance?"

"Sure thing."

Buck waited until she was gone to say, "Raine, I'm trying to help you out, here. I just want you to be careful."

"Careful of what, for heaven's sake?" Now that Effie's famous french fries were mere milliseconds away, I was running out of patience for this conversation. I squeezed a perfect puddle of ketchup on the side of my plate. "Andy is not coming here. You and your FBI pals are being paranoid for nothing. He has no reason to come back here. The whole thing is stupid."

"He has," Buck said gravely, "a hundred and thirty-two million reasons to come back here. And you know it as well as I do."

Chapter Six

Andy Fontana first ran afoul of the law at age eight. His crime: chicken theft. He came before Judge Stockton, who, upon learning the full story, was inclined to dismiss the charges as long as the property was returned forthwith. This, however, the indignant young man refused to do.

It seems that the chicken in question had a mangled foot. Andy had "stolen" it just as its owner was preparing to lay its head on the chopping block. He refused to return the chicken, which was getting around just fine on one foot, to a certain death. My father therefore issued an order of restitution, to be paid at the rate of ten cents a week, until the full purchase price of the chicken—valued at that time at five dollars and twenty-five cents—was paid. Even though the farmer in question lost his chicken houses to a fire later that spring and went out of business, Andy never missed a payment.

That's the kind of story that the newspapers didn't bother to print when the accusations started flying, although I told it to more than one reporter. Guess it wasn't sexy enough. Guess it didn't exactly fit in with their picture of a cold-blooded terrorist. Or maybe it was just that chickens don't sell papers.

My dad really liked Andy, who was being raised by his grandparents after his mother ran off and his father, a long-haul truck driver, fell asleep at the wheel in Minneapolis and went off a bridge. As a matter of fact, it was my father who gave the eight-year-old boy the job—mucking out our horse stalls every day after school and on Saturday mornings for fifty cents a week—that enabled him to pay off his debt to society. I used to sit on the rails and give orders, because mucking out the stalls was customarily my job, feeling all smug and superior until I realized that Andy was not only doing my job; he was also getting my allowance.

And then, as soon as Andy learned my nickname was "Rainbow," he took all the remaining starch out of my collar by whistling "Somewhere Over the Rainbow" until I picked up the nearest solid object and heaved it at him. Even as an adult, whenever he wanted to needle me or tease me or just get me off my high horse, he'd croon that stupid song until I beat him with a pillow or chased him around the room trying to choke him, which always ended in a laughing wrestling match, which always ended in something else.

Anyway, that's how Andy and I met, and it didn't take long before we were friends. His passion for the woods and thickets of our mountain wilderness was equaled only by my own, and he was smart too. He knew the name of every plant that grew on the hillside and what it was good for and what Indian lore was attached to it and how to "put by" what was needed of it for hard times. He knew the secret caves of the fox and the place where the bobcat had hidden her cubs. And if my mother had known of half the places we climbed and slid down and crawled through during our wild growing-up days, I don't think she would have ever slept a wink.

For reasons I'm not sure I ever understood, Buck and Andy were friends too. Here was this strange little orphan kid, always wandering around in the woods, needing a haircut and never caring that his jeans were baggy and his shirt was miss-buttoned, and there was the Super-Cool Dude, destined to be a football star, in his Air Jordans and his form-fitting 501's and his thick mane of gold-brown hair that even then turned the heads of females of all ages... Who knew? Maybe it had something to do with Eagle Scouts, one of those exclusive no-girls-allowed things that I never could fathom and always resented.

I know that Andy's grandparents made him join the Scouts as part of some kind of deal—I think in return for the 1978 Chevy he eventually received when he was sixteen—even though he never tired of telling me how lame Scouts was. Buck, who inherited Scouts just like he inherited Sunday school and 4-H, and who was accustomed to excelling at everything, was constantly skunked by Andy. Instead of beating him up, like most boys would have done, he started learning from him and became Andy's best friend. And that pretty much sums up Buck's character.

In case I didn't mention the fact that my character could have used some strengthening back in those days, the guy I eventually fell for was the one with the most shiny armor: Buck Lawson, the boy every girl wanted. The first time Buck broke my heart, Andy was the one who dried my tears and actually got us back together.

Buck and I were an on-and-off item all through high school, but my friendship with Andy — indeed, my love for him, though I didn't know that's what it was back then — never wavered.

Less than five percent of all graduates of Hansonville High School went on to college. Buck, Andy and I were three of the lucky ones. Buck got a football scholarship, and Andy got an academic scholarship, to North Carolina State. My mother, a graduate of Converse College, and my father, whose alma mater was William and Mary, both thought they had dibs on my educational future. But I chose North Carolina State, partly because I wanted to assert my independence, but mostly because Andy kept raving about the Department of Environmental Resources there and because I couldn't think of anything better than to spend my college years studying the wilderness that I loved.

The summer before we all were to pack up for Raleigh, Buck's forty-two-year-old father had a heart attack and died. Buck, it seemed, grew up overnight. It was a somber eighteen-year-old who decided playing football wasn't nearly as important as taking care of his family, especially since the criminal justice degree he wanted was just as easily obtained from the Cullowhee campus, which was an easy day trip from home. His sacrifice was noble, and as disappointed as I was to see our dreams of four years in Raleigh go up in smoke, I understood, and I admired him for it.

Then he made his big mistake. What did I need to go off to college for, anyway? he insisted. If I stayed around home and got a job, we could get married in a couple of years and even have a little money saved for a house.

Most of the girls in my graduating class would have been thrilled with an offer like that, would have rushed home to start planning the wedding with their mamas so fast, Buck wouldn't even have seen them go. But I was not most girls. I had ambitions, plans, dreams. Buck knew that—or at least I thought he did. He respected me for that...or at least I thought he did.

The conversation deteriorated from there. He accused me of thinking I was too good to be his wife. I accused him of being a chauvinist pig. I think I ended up punching him in the face, and he ended up calling me a spoiled rich kid. I left for Raleigh in September without ever speaking to Buck again.

As is often typical with unpopular kids, campus life gave Andy a chance to blossom in a way that Hansonville never had. He was on the school paper and, in sophomore year, actually started an underground paper of his own. He was on this committee and that. He made speeches on the quad and hung out with a much more interesting class of people than I did. All of this grazed the periphery of my campus self-absorption until, at the beginning of our junior year, I realized that I was actually interesting to people who mattered simply by virtue of knowing

Andy.

I took a second look at Andy and realized that I had been falling in love with him for about ten years.

My birthday came three weeks after we had started seriously dating. Andy presented me with a single cupcake topped with a candle and a small wrapped box. Inside the cupcake was a tiny metal key, which he told me was the key to his heart. Inside the box was a larger key, which fit the lock on his apartment door.

I moved in the next day. I still have the miniature key, which I attached to a charm bracelet and wore almost every day until I married Buck.

It wasn't hard to be drawn into Andy's passions, his causes, his absolute conviction that he, and only he, could save the world from industrial pollution, global warming and deforestation. After all, we believed in the same things. We championed the same causes. We came from the same place.

I knew he was involved with People for a Clean Planet—PCP, as it was called, with the double entendre fully acknowledged and intended—from the beginning. And, if truth be known, the only thing that kept me out of the organization—and therefore, as it turned out, out of prison—was a heavy class load. For Andy, academics were something he did in his spare time, and he was smart enough to get away with it; I struggled to keep up with my course work and still barely maintained an average that would keep my parents writing the checks.

PCP had a mission statement that sounded

solid and an ideology I could support: All they wanted to do was to save this planet's natural resources for the next generation. Little did I know at the time that they had no problem with saving the planet by killing off a few of the planet's most conspicuous consumers: human beings.

By the time PCP was cited for possible involvement in the sinking of an oil freighter off the coast of Alaska, Andy was so deeply entangled with them that he couldn't have extricated himself even if he had wanted to. I will never forget the cold look in his eyes when he said, "What's one stinking freighter in the overall scheme of things? Someday history will call us heroes."

Us. He had said us.

Thirteen crewmen had been aboard that ship. None had perished, but all of them might have. I started seeing the radical environmentalist movement in a new light and started to understand why they called them ecoterrorists.

I begged Andy to walk away from PCP. He accused me of being my father's daughter, brainwashed by the right-wing establishment and too afraid of getting into trouble to take a risk. That stung. No, that stabbed.

I went home for Christmas, and when I went back to Raleigh in January it was not to Andy's off-campus apartment. In June, we both graduated. Fourteen months later I was Mrs. Buck Lawson, and Andy was the object of a national manhunt.

During that year after graduation the activities of People for a Clean Planet seemed to escalate, although, according to all reports, its actual numbers were diminishing. A stolen oil tanker was parked on a bridge under construction and detonated. A fertilizer warehouse burned down. A bomb was planted in a research laboratory, and a right-wing newspaper office burned down. But it wasn't until the Memorial Day bombing of the offices of the petrochemical manufacturer that people actually died. And that was the beginning of the end for People for a Clean Planet.

The last straggling members of PCP were rounded up—all except Andy. Much to the federal investigators' frustration, the one thing they wanted most, next to Andy, was never recovered: PCP's reported 132-million-dollar treasury, most of which had been acquired in a series of bank robberies to which the members of the group who were already in custody eventually confessed. Those same members, who might be called anything but stupid, also insisted that Andy Fontana, who was by that time so far from the reach of the long arm of the law that most people believed he was dead, was the only person who knew where that money was.

Of course, that's the kind of thing of which legends are made. The theory was that Andy had somehow made it back to his old stomping grounds and hidden, buried or otherwise disposed of 132 million dollars in ill-gotten gains. For years afterward a good percentage of my search and rescue work was related to treasure hunters who were certain they would be the ones to unearth the fortune where all others had failed and who, instead, usually found themselves hopelessly lost, trapped in a gorge or hanging from a precipice on the side of a mountain.

I don't suppose I have to point out that one of

the issues upon which Buck and I disagreed most vehemently was the eventual fate of that money. In my opinion, the cash had been transferred to some offshore account long before Andy ever became involved. Even if he had had access to it, which I very much doubted, the last place he would try to hide it was here. And even if he had wanted to hide it here, I could never see how he might have managed it in the short space between the time he was accused of the bombing and the time he disappeared. I was always surprised and annoyed when Buck brought up the subject as a viable theory.

I said, "Come on, Buck, are we really going to go there again?" Carefully I sliced the giant hamburger in half, trying not to spill pickles or lettuce in the process. "Just answer me this, then. If Andy really had buried a hundred and thirty two million out in the Woods somewhere, why wouldn't he have come back for it before now?"

Buck looked as though he actually might answer that, but just then the radio hooked on his shoulder epaulet began to squawk static. He held up a finger as a placeholder and excused himself. I heard him reply, "Yeah, this is unit eight," as he pushed his chair back and left the table.

He didn't leave the room, just walked far enough away that my meal would not be disturbed by whatever gruesome details were coming in over the airwaves. I heard the tinny voice of the dispatcher and some of Buck's replies, but I wasn't interested in trying to figure out what they were saying. I dipped a golden french fry into the ketchup and enjoyed a moment of pure nirvana.

Then I heard Buck say, approaching the table again, "No, don't make him come all the way out there. I've got Raine right here, and we're three minutes away."

I paused with my second french fry halfway to my mouth and began to shake my head vehemently. I didn't know what he had just volunteered me for, but I wanted no part of it. I was wearing my good sandals, and my shirt was dry-clean only, and he had promised me supper.

"No way," I said as he signed off. "Leave me out of it. You're the cop on duty. I'm just a girl trying to finish her burger." I stuffed the french fry in my mouth and picked up another.

Buck snagged a take-out box from the hostess stand and shoved it at me. "There's a bear got himself trapped in a truck over at the construction sight, and some fool is taking potshots at it."

I said, "Oh, terrific." I scooped the contents of my plate into the take-out box on the run and called to Effie, "Put it on Buck's bill," as I hurried after him out the door.

I drove my own car, but with Buck's sirens blaring it probably took us less than three minutes to reach the excitement. I had hoped all the noise and lights would have scared the bear back into the woods, but from the excited pointing and gesturing that came from the knot of men that had gathered midway up the mud slope where the construction equipment was parked, I could see that we were not to be so lucky.

I parked behind Buck and we both got out at the same time, but he had to grab my arm to keep me from charging up to the stranger who was sighting down the barrel of a rifle. I opened my mouth to yell, but Buck's voice was louder than mine.

"Excuse me, sir."

That got the shooter's finger off the trigger, but he did not look inclined to lower the weapon as he looked around at Buck.

Buck continued in an easy, friendly manner as we approached, "Unless I'm mistaken, bear is out of season, so you'll probably want to put that rifle down, if you don't mind."

"He's in my goddamn truck!" shouted the man and turned his attention back to his rifle sights. "He's tearing it apart!"

In one swift stride Buck had his hand on the man's forearm, and the rifle came down. Buck said, still very politely, "When an officer of the law tells you to put the weapon down, sir, it's usually a real good idea to listen to him. Besides that, I've got Officer Stockton here of the DNR, and if you think that bear is mad, you sure don't want to piss her off."

I barely spared Buck an askance glance; an officer I was not, at least not at present, but with or without the authority I surely would have done some bodily harm if the guy had wounded that bear. When I saw that the rifle was safely out of the offender's hands, I turned my attention to the pickup truck some fifty yards away. I could definitely see why the fellow was upset.

The driver's door was sagging off its hinges, the front windshield was starred, and upholstery stuffing littered the ground. The truck rocked and creaked with movement, and even as I watched, a distinctive off-pitch roar of annoyance made everyone take a startled step back, even me.

Though it was barely dusk, all I could see inside the truck was a huge dark form; no way of telling how big he was, or whether he was hurt or wedged in there. There was no doubt it was a bear, though. The odor of wild musk and sour meat was unmistakable, and it clung to the hillside. There was an earthmover and a backhoe between us and the truck so I didn't think any of us were in any immediate danger, but bears can move awfully fast when they have a mind to.

Someone was saying, "Thanks for getting here so quick, Deputy. I'm the one that called 911 from my cell phone."

Another added, "We just went to town for a bite to eat, you know, and Micky here, he rode with us but then wanted to stop back by the site and get a six-pack he'd left in his truck, before we went on to the motel. Good thing we did, too, cause when we got back here that thing was going to town—"

"Got every tire on the place," interrupted another excitedly. I noticed he had a camera and had apparently already snapped a few pictures. Well, it's not every day you see a bear in a pickup. "I never heard of a bear doing that, did you?"

"'Bout tore up that 'cat, over yonder," added somebody else, and it took me a moment to realize he meant the Bobcat—a piece of earthmoving equipment, not the live specimen. "Looks like I got the day off tomorrow."

"First we thought it was a bunch of kids, vandals, you know. Then we saw Micky's truck."

I said, "So the bear was in the truck when you got here?"

"Hell, yeah, he was. That's when I went and

grabbed my gun. Got off a couple of shots but didn't hit nothing."

"Lucky for you," I told him, scowling. "Aside from a hefty fine and a jail sentence, if you think you've got problems now, you don't want to see how quick a bear can lose his temper when he's wounded. What kind of food did you leave in that truck anyway?'

The man, whose name apparently was Micky, looked as though he wanted to mouth off to me, but somebody else supplied, grinning, "Hell, that truck of Micky's is nothing but a garbage can. What kind of food don't he have in there? I always told you it was going to get you in trouble," he added, elbowing Micky, "but I figured it would be with the health department."

"Is that what he's after?" The man who spoke addressed Buck, like they always do, but I was the one who answered.

"Probably."

Buck asked me, "What do you think? It'll take Rick about half an hour to get out here with a tranq gun. Then I figure we'll have to call the fire department to get the bear out of the truck."

The bear roared again and the truck shook. Micky, without his gun, wasn't half as brave as he had been formerly, and he took several running steps backward.

I said, frowning, "Hold on a minute. He might come out on his own."

"Looks like he's stuck in there to me."

"Maybe."

Buck turned to one of the men. "Where're you boys from?"

They said they were from over in Gastonia,

South Carolina, and while they were talking I went back to my car and got the take-out carton. I tore off the lid, and the aroma of hamburger and french fries was sweet enough to make me leave home for, much less abandon the garbage of some half-torn-up pickup truck.

Although not normally aggressive, bears are certainly nothing to fool around with, as the average person could easily determine from the size of their teeth and claws. I'm not saying I wasn't jumpy as I edged around the construction equipment toward the truck, always trying to keep something big between me and the bear, and if the animal had been out in the open I never would have been so brave. But I had no doubt I could outrun the creature before he could wriggle out of the truck window, and as soon as I set the open take-out box on the ground about six feet away from the truck, that's exactly what I did.

We had to wait only about five minutes, although it seemed much longer than that. By the time the bear, roaring with frustration, was halfway out the door, all the construction workers were inside their vehicle, and Buck and I were hiding behind the open door of the patrol car, ready to spring inside at a moment's notice. But as I had hoped, the bear was far more interested in the hamburger than in anything else in his surroundings. When he finally squeezed out of the truck he made short work of my dinner.

"Good God almighty," Buck said softly beside me, "that is one big son of a bitch, isn't it?"

For a moment I was too overwhelmed to do anything but nod. He was magnificent. Rarely do human beings get the chance to be within a few dozen feet of a creature bigger and stronger than they are; it is a humbling experience. The bear might not have been five hundred pounds, as Mrs. Tucker had insisted, but even when he stood on all fours, the curve of his back was level with the door handle of the truck, and from the angle at which I was watching he seemed almost as long as the half-bed pickup. How he had managed to pack himself into the cab of that truck I couldn't imagine.

He shredded the box with one swipe of his paw, grumbled and shook himself so that his blue-black coat shimmered in the last rays of the sun. Then he turned and ambled up the hill. I don't think anyone breathed or moved until the sound of crashing in the thicket faded away.

"Wow," I said reverently, straightening up. "That was really something."

"Sure was," Buck agreed, grinning at me. He clapped me on the shoulder in a congratulatory way. "The girl of the hour. Guess your daddy wouldn't think all that money he spent on your college education was wasted now."

"Don't call me a girl."

"Yes, ma'am."

The other men were getting cautiously out of the truck, and Buck said, "Now the fun part starts. The paperwork."

"Well, I guess my job here is done. Thanks for supper."

"How about a rain check?"

"Don't know if I can stand the excitement. And I get a lot more to eat when I eat at home."

Buck said, "Hey, Rainey." He was looking at the dump truck that was parked up against the side of the hill, which was now sagging on four flat tires. He kept his voice casual, but low. "Did you get a look at those tires?"

I followed his gaze. "Can't say that I did."

"The Bobcat too. See how it's all banged up on the side? Do you think the bear could have done that?"

I hesitated. I couldn't quite tell whether he was asking my professional opinion, and if he was, I wanted to be careful. "I've seen bears do some weird things. I watched one pick up a hundred-pound metal compost drum one time, roll it off into the woods and smash it open with his paws."

"Yeah, but look. All the tires on every truck are slashed. What's he got against tires?"

I shrugged. "Couldn't say, Buck. But he was awfully methodical, wasn't he?"

Buck gave a thoughtful grunt of agreement and took out his note pad. "I'll call you later."

"You do that."

"Hey." As I turned toward the car he cupped his hand behind my neck and brushed my cheek with a kiss. He smiled at me. "Thanks."

I tried to look annoyed, but it was hard. "Not in front of the guys," I said, shrugging away as I inclined my head toward the construction workers. But by then I was smiling too.

"Take care of yourself."

I returned a muffled chuckle and jerked my thumb toward Micky, who had gotten up the nerve to inspect his mangled truck and was throwing a tantrum that would have put the bear to shame—kicking tires, flinging his hat on the ground and cursing at the top of his lungs.

"You too," I said.

It was as I was climbing into my car that I noticed the glint of something on the ground, just a few inches behind my front tire. I probably wouldn't have noticed it at all had not the light from the courtesy lamp on the driver's side door reflected off the sliver of metal as the door swung open. I stretched down to pick it up. It was a gold chain, broken at the clasp, with a gold crucifix attached to it.

I recognized it immediately, of course. Manny, the Mexican fellow who had stolen my dog's affections this afternoon, had obviously lost it on the job when he returned to the construction site. I lifted my hand toward the workers Buck was now interviewing and started to call out to one of them, then thought better of it.

This was a valuable piece of jewelry and I didn't know any of those guys. Buck hated this kind of babysitting work, and there was no point in bothering him with a lost-and-found job when I knew whom the item belonged to. Better to try to return it to its owner myself, or at least to find the construction foreman in the morning and hand it over to him. As I slipped the necklace into the change compartment of my wallet, it never once occurred to me that this might not be the right thing to do.

Why should it have?

I proceeded down the gravel-strewn slope and onto Valley Street at a slower-than-usual pace, partly because dark was coming on and the place where the carved-out construction road met the main road was on a dangerous curve, and partly because my eyes were still scanning the surrounding woods for the bear. I felt pretty sure he had hightailed it home, wherever home might be, but bears can be unpredictable creatures where food is concerned. And he had already been rewarded for his efforts twice tonight—once with my supper.

Had I been traveling at my usual confident speed, or if I hadn't been paying more attention to the surrounding countryside than to the road, I might have missed it. As it was, my headlights picked up the shape on the side of the road, half in and half out of the ditch. I had driven another hundred yards before my mind actually registered what I had seen. I slammed on the brakes, shifted into reverse and backed up, my pulse pounding in my temples, hoping against hope that I had not, in fact, seen what I knew I had seen.

I actually backed past the spot, and I thought I must have been mistaken after all. But no. When I turned my attention away from the rearview mirror and looked forward, I caught a suggestion of a lumpy shape in the dry grass, a scrap of fabric out of place. I eased the car forward until the headlights shone like spotlights on the body on the side of the road.

Somehow I remembered to put the car in park and to set the emergency brake. When I flung open the door the awkward angle at which I had stopped caused it to fly out of my hand and I almost fell out of the car. My throat was dry and my stomach hurt and my knees were like rubber. I stumbled and slid on loose gravel as I scrambled down the slope, catching myself on one hand. I halted, heart pounding, about three feet away from where the body lay at a broken angle facedown in the weeds.

Wilderness training has taught me what to do in an emergency, and I had, unfortunately, seen more than one dead body in my life. But none of that made it any easier to approach the prone figure and to drop to my knees beside it.

His hair was dark, and so was the skin of his arms beneath the short-sleeved plaid shirt he wore. His jeans were scuffed and torn and one shoe was missing. One leg was hyper-extended away from his body at the knee and the material covering it was dark with blood.

Death is unmistakable. There is no stillness like it, no silence to compare to it. I knew this man was dead. But compassion, or perhaps some faint stubborn hope, compelled me to stretch out a hand and search for a carotid pulse.

The flesh was cold but still relatively supple, which a faraway part of my brain registered to mean that death had occurred recently. When I moved my fingers, still searching futilely for a pulse I knew was not there, his head shifted and rolled loosely on broken, disconnected vertebrae, revealing a portion of his face.

I gasped and jerked back. "Oh, God," I whispered, staring. "Oh, no."

I scrambled to my feet, clawed my way back to the car and pulled open the door. I couldn't find my phone, couldn't remember whether I had even brought it with me. All I could think to do was to blow the horn and to keep leaning on it until Buck arrived.

Chapter Seven

His name was Manuel Rodriguez," Buck said, nodding toward the officer who was interviewing the construction workers near a patrol car. "He was in charge of the Mexican crew at the work site."

The construction workers looked as though they had had more than enough excitement for one night. Standing in the circle of whirling blue lights, they kept shoving their hands through their hair and shaking their heads. Even Micky, whose biggest problem a few minutes ago had been a mangled truck, looked stunned and overwhelmed.

"I know," I said. Despite the warm night, I rubbed my bare arms to keep the gooseflesh down. "I mean I know that his name was Manny."

Buck looked at me curiously, and I explained, "He came over to pet Cisco this morning at the feed store. He has a golden retriever at home."

"Looks like a hit-and-run to me. Must've just happened." I shot my eyes to his in alarm. "You mean while we were up there, just a few hundred yards away?"

He shrugged. "Maybe. The boys say they didn't see anything when they drove up, and we for damn sure didn't. Course, it would be hard to see the body in the ditch coming up the hill. Easier going down."

I remembered how I had missed seeing it when I backed up. My throat tight, I said, "You don't suppose one of them"—I nodded toward the construction workers—"hit him on their way up the hill just now, do you? When they came back from supper?"

Buck shook his head. "There would be damage to their vehicle. And all of them alibi each other."

"What about Micky's truck?" I insisted. "There was plenty of damage there, and maybe not all of it was from the bear."

I knew I was stretching, and Buck confirmed it. "Yeah, but all the damage is in the wrong place. From what we can tell, Rodriguez was hit from behind and thrown into the ditch. Whoever did it is going to have damage on the right front. Pretty noticeable too."

I watched as the EMTs loaded the sheet-covered body into the back of the ambulance. No light, no sirens. No need for them now.

I shook my head slowly. "How could anyone do that? Just hit somebody and drive away?"

"Most of the time they don't even know," Buck said. "The way these big trucks and SUVs are built, they're riding along with the CD player going, talking on the phone, it's getting dark, they feel a thump, think maybe it's a deer or a dog, slow down and look back, don't see anything…" He shrugged. "Maybe they've had a few beers, don't even slow down. Most of the time they don't even know what happened till they read about it in the paper."

I said softly, hugging my arms, "My God."

"We'll put the word out to all the body shops and garages in the area to be on the lookout for a damaged right front fender. Or maybe the guy will turn himself in when he hears about it on the radio."

I looked at him. "Do they ever do that?"

"Sometimes."

Another vehicle pulled off the road and parked in the dirt, and a harried-looking man got out. "That must be the construction foreman," Buck said. "I need to talk to him. Why don't you go on home? I'll call you if I need anything else."

I drew in a breath to protest, and then let it go in a sigh. "It's just... he seemed nice, you know?"

Buck gripped my shoulder in a brief, sympathetic gesture, then left.

I waited until the ambulance pulled away, and then I got into my car and drove slowly home. When I got home it was fully dark. I flipped on the light switch as I walked in the front door and stood in the center of a scene that, in terms of the amount of wanton destruction, was not that much different from the one the bear had left behind at the construction site. This was, without a doubt, the last thing in the world I needed.

Sofa cushions were scattered across the floor. An end table was overturned. Magazines were shredded. Lampshades were askew. Majesty, my faithful watch collie, stood in her crate barking insistently. The door of Mischief's crate was open, and she was nowhere to be seen.

The average person would have suspected a

break-in, and in fact, with my nerves still raw from the events of the evening, my hand was on the telephone to dial 911 when I noticed the open door of the crate. All the dogs except Cisco are always crated when I'm out of the house, and Cisco would have been too had it not been for his phobia of being locked up. He usually did okay when left alone in the house, though I suspected a secret propensity to take a snooze on my bed when I wasn't around. This kind of rampage was entirely out of character for him.

Magic, the other Aussie, was standing hopefully at the door to her crate, tailless butt wagging enthusiastically, but Mischief had apparently slid the bolt lock free and made a break for it. Could she have actually done that? I questioned the possibility for only a minute.

A lot of people don't realize how dexterous Australian shepherds are. They can use their paws like hands to cup small objects, climb sheer surfaces, and manipulate items from one surface to another. This, in combination with an almost Houdini-like agility and the unsettling cleverness that is common to all the herding breeds, makes it a wise policy to put nothing past them. The hurricane-like chaos that had attacked my home had her paw prints all over it.

I said, "Majesty, quiet!" and raced to the kitchen, while Majesty, who had more to say about the subject than she could possibly contain, continued to bark indignantly from the living room.

There they were, the culprits. Grinning up at me, Cisco lay on the floor in the middle of a spilled canister of flour, a chewed-through box of dog biscuits between his paws, flour on his head, flour on his nose, flour dust swishing back and forth with the happy wagging of his tail. There was sugar in the sink and coffee grounds on the counter-top. An overturned vase of purple hydrangeas dripped a puddle on the floor, making a lovely glue out of the flour. In the center of the kitchen table sat Mischief, licking the platter that had once contained the peanut butter cookies which, for lack of a better alternative, I had hoped to make my supper.

The overturned flour and sugar canisters I could understand, but I couldn't for the life of me figure out how Mischief had climbed to the second row of cabinets, opened the door and pulled out the box of dog biscuits for Cisco.

But such is life with dogs. There were times when I honestly thought a bear might be easier.

There was even more bedlam upstairs: toilet paper unrolled, bed rumpled, underwear trailing out of drawers, the contents of my vanity and jewelry box overturned where some dog had apparently tugged the table scarf on which they rested.

Of course I was furious. Of course I would have traded every one of them in for a stuffed cat if someone had made me an offer at that moment. But as exasperating, time consuming and downright aggravating as they can be, dogs have one singular quality that makes up for all the rest: They live entirely in the moment. Most of the time, they require us to do the same. Less than an hour ago I had knelt in the dry grass at the side of the road and touched a dead man's broken neck. Now I wasn't thinking about anything except how to get flour-glue paw prints out of my mother's Oriental carpet.

It was after ten by the time I finished cleaning up, scolding dogs, shampooing the flour out of Cisco's fur and letting Magic and Majesty, who were the only dogs I could be sure were completely guiltless, out into the back for a nice, long run. This had definitely been a day I hoped not to repeat soon, and I was dragging myself off to bed when I happened to notice that the light on the answering machine was blinking.

The temptation was to ignore it, but when you're in business you can't do that. Sometimes people call the kennel number and get the machine, then try to catch me at home. I played the first message.

"Hey, Rainbow; it's Uncle Roe. I'm calling you from home." I glanced at the timer on the machine; 7:45 p.m., a half hour before I had discovered the body and half his force had been called out to investigate.

"I guess Buck has talked to you by now, and that federal agent. Hell of a thing, huh? Here we've got an international fugitive headed this way, and my best tracker just happens to be his ex-girlfriend. Sure could use your help if he does happen to make it this far."

My uncle knew perfectly well that since I was not an employee of his department—or of any government agency at present, in fact—I was not authorized to track down dangerous criminals. This was just his way of voicing his frustration, and, oddly enough, of letting me know he was concerned about me.

"Anyhow," he went on, "Aunt Mart wants you

to come by for dinner after church on Sunday. Give her a call. Bye, now. Oh, she says you can bring that pretty dog she likes so much. Bye."

That made me smile. My aunt Mart was not much of an animal lover, but she did adore Majesty, who had earned her name with her long flowing coat and regal collie expression. At present Majesty was badly in need of a good brushing and a toenail trim, but it might have been worth the trouble to spruce her up for Aunt Mart's peach cobbler. Unfortunately, I would be at the dog show on Saturday and Sunday, so peach cobbler would have to wait. I made a note to call Aunt Mart tomorrow.

I hit the delete button, and suddenly I remembered, for no reason at all, the crucifix that I had found at the construction site and dropped into my change purse. I said, "Damn!" Cisco, who had heard me use that word once too often tonight, pricked up his still-damp ears and thumped his tail uncertainly. I punched a speed dial code on the telephone.

Aunt Mart answered on the second ring.

"Hi, Aunt Mart; it's me," I said in a rush. "I'm sorry it's late; were you in bed?"

"Oh, sweetheart, you know me, just sitting up in bed watching that cop show on TV. What are you doing up and about?"

"Uncle Roe called earlier. I thought I'd try to catch him at home."

"Oh, they called him in to work." Her voice lowered a fraction. "A terrible thing, dear. A hit-and-run out on Valley Street. No one we know, though."

I said, "I know. I'm the one who found the

body." I explained as quickly as I could, amidst her gasps and murmurs of sympathy and surprise. "I didn't know they were going to call Uncle Roe, though," I added. "Buck seemed to think it was pretty cut-and-dried."

"Oh, it wasn't Buck who called," Aunt Mart said. "It was that FBI fellow."

I scowled at the phone. "About a hit-and-run?"

"Darling, I don't know. And the less I know about Roe's work, the better I sleep at night. Do you want me to tell him you called?"

I hesitated. It was late; I had to be up for a five o'clock tracking class, and what difference would a few hours make? I would drop the necklace by the office in the morning. I said, "No, that's okay. I'll probably see him tomorrow anyway. I just wanted to check in."

"You coming to dinner Sunday? Roe will probably have to work, with this schedule they've got him on, but that's no reason to let a perfectly good pot roast go to waste."

I explained, with genuine regret, about the dog show. "Oh, are you taking that pretty collie?"

"Not this time. It's not that kind of show."

"Well, win some ribbons anyway." She sounded a little disappointed. I've always suspected that Aunt Mart secretly regards all this running and jumping and tramping through the woods with dogs as unladylike, whereas trotting a beautiful collie around a conformation ring would be much more suitable. "Maybe I'll make the pot roast next Sunday."

"Get back to your TV show, Aunt Mart. I love you."

"Love you too, sweetheart. Take care of

yourself."

The message light was still blinking, indicating another call, and I pushed the playback button. It was Jim Peterson, one of my neighbors. "Hey, Raine. We got a little yellow lab over here; wonder if you might know where he came from. Wearing a red collar and a rabies tag, but no phone number."

I am a volunteer for Purebred Rescue, and one of the first rules of rescue is that you never turn your back on a dog in need, which is exactly how I ended up with Majesty, Mischief and Magic. I picked up the phone to return the call when the next message played.

"It's Jim Peterson again. Found the dog's owner. Some damn-fool tourist left it in the car while they went to take a picture of a waterfall or something, and it must've jumped out. Don't that beat all? Good thing they happened to see it in the yard when they drove by. Well, thanks anyway."

I blew out a breath of tired relief and replaced the receiver. I said, "Come on, guys, let's go to bed." I turned to start sorting the dogs into their various crates when the answering machine beep sounded again.

For a minute there was silence from the machine, and then the oddest thing. A ringtone began to play a sweet, electronic, heartbreakingly familiar tune. It was "Somewhere Over the Rainbow."

For a moment I just stared at the machine, trying to make some connection between my uncle's voice—"Hello, Rainbow"—and this tune. But there was no connection. That's when I understood, and my knees went weak.

Without thinking, I stabbed the delete button, and then I stood there, staring at the machine, hardly daring to breathe.

It was a joke. A stupid, sick joke. Of course it was. It had to be. But who would do such a thing?

There was only one person I could think of, and he was in no position to be joking.

But that was crazy. It was a joke. Or a coincidence.

Yes, that was it. It had to be. Just someone with a collection of ringtones who was teasing me with my nickname. It was a harmless prank, that was all.

It had been a long, hard, horrible day, and a stupid joke like this was no way to end it. By the time I wearily climbed the stairs for bed, I had almost convinced myself.

As a general rule, life begins around here each day at six a.m., rain or shine, summer, winter and in between. It doesn't matter if I've been up every two hours with a sick dog or out all night beating the bushes for a lost tourist or tossing and turning with wild dreams about bears and bobcats being chased by the FBI. The only exception to this ungodly wakeup hour is when the day starts at four thirty a.m. for tracking class, or five thirty a.m. for an agility trial.

Once the day starts, once the first bark echoes across the hills, it goes full tilt, without a break, until the last crate door is closed. I therefore treasure every precious moment that my head is in contact with my pillow. And the dogs who have earned the privilege of sharing my home have learned that no good thing ever comes of waking me before the first note of country-and-western music sounds from the clock radio on my night table.

As it happened, the next morning was one of the four thirty a.m. days. When Cisco's low, rumbling growl dragged me out of my restless bobcat dreams and my slitted eyes showed me a digital clock reading of four o'clock, the first thing I did was to lob a pillow in his general direction. Cisco, due to his crate phobia, is the only dog who doesn't have his own secure den for the night. The upside of that—for him—is that he gets to sleep on the rug beside my bed. The downside of that—for me— is moments like this.

Of course, throwing the pillow at Cisco was a bad idea, because that only incited him to leap to his feet and start barking wildly. That in turn woke Majesty, Mischief and Magic, who joined in the chorus from downstairs. I snapped, "Quiet!" with my eyes squeezed tightly closed and my head buried under the other pillow. The "quiet" command almost always works with Cisco, who is not a big barker, and almost never works with any of the other dogs, who live to bark. This time it had virtually no effect at all.

It took less than thirty seconds for me to realize this, and I sat up in bed. "Damn it, Cisco, quiet!" I tried again, putting more force into my voice. In the shadowed dawn I could see Cisco half turn his head toward me, and then he went back to the closed bedroom door, feet braced, head down, barking with steadily increasing alarm.

Something was outside.

Anyone who lives with a dog learns to read the tone of his various barks. Otherwise the average homeowner would be rushing to the door with a shotgun fifteen or twenty times a day. There is the squirrel-in-the-bird-feeder bark and the cat-crossing-the-lawn bark and the deer-in-the-garden bark and the UPS-truck bark, all of which relay essential, if not precisely urgent, information from dog to human.

Then there is this bark. It was the kind of bark that would prompt the average homeowner, had she not been half asleep and cursing the fact that it was four o'clock in the morning, to go in search of the shotgun.

I swung out of bed, hit the alarm off button on the clock radio, and stuffed my feet into a pair of battered sneakers that I kept nearby in case of emergency trips to the backyard. Cisco, growing increasingly agitated, bounded to the window, still barking, and put his paws on the sill. I could see that his hackles were up. I grabbed the flashlight that I kept beside the bed, and he raced to the door. The dogs in their crates downstairs were hysterical, and now I could hear the muffled sounds of the kennel dogs starting to join in.

As I opened the bedroom door, I thought Cisco was going to fall down the stairs in his hurry to get to the bottom of them. He scrambled down, his white-feathered tail tracing mad cartwheels in the air, and I hurried after him, holding on to the banister. On my way past, I tapped the nearest crate with the flat of my hand and repeated loudly, "Quiet!" which gave me an approximately two-second pause in the cacophony. Cisco raced toward the back door.

I always closed up the dog door at night—a sensible precaution when you live in an area where raccoons, possums, stray cats and skunks can learn to operate the swinging vinyl partition as easily as a dog can—so Cisco was thwarted on his first attempt to chase down whatever it was that had caused all the excitement He put his paws up on the window insert and barked again, and that was when I noticed that the security lights were on.

The area closest to the house in the back is fenced for the dogs, and Buck had installed the motion-sensing lights so that I could easily see the dogs when I let them out at night. The lights should not have been triggered unless something had approached the fence.

I told Cisco sharply, "Sit!" and, because this is one command that I have reinforced repeatedly and consistently since he was eight weeks old, Cisco sat. He didn't like it, though. He whined and licked his lips and shuffled his feet anxiously, and because I could tell that instinct might override training at any moment, I held on to his collar to keep him behind me while I eased open the back door and edged outside.

I was right about Cisco's impulse control. As soon as I released his collar, he charged past me for the gate. And even though I could clearly see that the gate was closed, my heart still skipped a beat as he threw himself against it so hard that his back feet left the ground.

I switched on the high-powered flashlight and scanned the shadows at the perimeter of the property, certain that whatever was out there, or had been out there, was either long gone or incredibly stupid. Every dog in the kennel was barking now, not to mention the three dogs in the house. Security lights were on at every corner of the kennel building and on the back side of the house.

Nonetheless, as I swept the flashlight beam across the edge of the yard where it faded into the woods, just this side of a wildflower patch that was fast being overtaken by weeds, I caught a glimpse of something: a lighter shape against the shadows. A deer? A coyote?

A man?

It seemed to hesitate for a moment at the edge of the flashlight beam, almost as though it were too arrogant, or too unconcerned, to care about discovery. And then, as my light beam quickly swept back for a better look, it seemed to turn and melt into the shadows of the woods that surrounded it. Though I played the beam over the area where the shape had disappeared for another solid minute, I did not pick up so much as a glimpse of a phosphorescent eye.

Coyote, I decided uneasily, and took Cisco's collar again. "Come on, fellow. That's enough."

This time, apparently satisfied that he had chased the intruder away, Cisco was ready to obey. He turned and trotted back toward the house, grinning and waving his plumed tail proudly. At the door I turned back and once again swept the woods with my beam. But there was nothing there.

Tracking class is held in a different field or wooded lot each month, so that the dogs don't become overly familiar with the terrain. A dedicated member of the class gets there early—

we rotate that duty too—and carefully lays out a track marked with small orange flags. In the winter and early spring, before the woods become too snaky, we practice rescue operations with a live "victim," who hides in a gully or buries him- or herself in the snow. Sometimes we have to drive as long as two hours to get to the site of the class before dawn, when the rising sun and increasing animal and human population corrupt the scent of the tracks.

Today I was lucky on two counts: I had to drive only twenty-five minutes to get to the site, and I did not have to lay the track. But by the time I calmed down the kennel dogs, made a thermos full of coffee, dressed, filled my pack and spent fifteen minutes looking for the peanut butter—which I never did find—I was running late.

The peanut butter was to keep Mischief occupied while Cisco and I were busy in tracking class. A little peanut butter smeared inside a sterilized marrowbone or a rubber toy will keep a dog interested for hours, and I planned to leave Mischief in the car while Cisco and I were working. We would pass a fenced baseball field on the way back from class, a perfect place to practice some of the agility moves Mischief would be using at the upcoming show, and it's always important to practice familiar behaviors in a strange place before a show.

So by the time I packed my portable agility jumps and tunnel, Cisco's tracking harness and my backpack, a couple of toys for Mischief and a can of squeeze-cheese in lieu of peanut butter, I was ten minutes late and hadn't had any breakfast. Apparently the box of toaster pastries that I had intended to buy last week had never made it into the cart. Or maybe Mischief had helped herself to those last night as well as to the plate of cookies.

I ploughed down the nearly empty highway in the dark, both dogs fastened into their seat belts in the backseat, and tuned in to the local radio station for a weather forecast. I caught the tail end of "Twenty percent chance of rain tomorrow, high eighty-two," before the tinny-voiced broadcaster turned to the news.

"City council met last night to discuss the rezoning of a section of Highway 6 from agricultural to commercial. Lionel Reems, who requested the rezoning, said his property would be more valuable if the zoning was changed. Chuck Williams, president of the Hansonville City Council, said they would not be granting any more rezoning requests until September, and that the matter would be tabled until then.

"The Hanover County Sheriff's Department responded to a complaint of vandalism at a construction site on Valley Street last night and discovered a large black bear had damaged several vehicles parked there. The amount of the destruction is in the thousands, according to a company spokesperson, and will delay completion of the project for about a week."

"Well, good for you, bear," I muttered and reached to turn off the radio.

"In other news, a man was found dead last evening, victim of an apparent hit-and-run. Manuel Rodriguez, thirty-five, who was employed by the Steven Blake Construction Company out of South Carolina, was apparently walking north along Valley Street last evening when he was struck by a vehicle from behind. Police are seeking information on a vehicle with right front side damage, and anyone who was in the vicinity of Valley Street last night between six and eight o'clock is asked to contact the Hanover County Sheriff's Department.

"Services for Pearlene Bryce, eighty-seven, will be held tomorrow at two o'clock at the First Calvary Baptist Church. There will be a visitation at Holmes Funeral Parlor tonight from seven to nine. Mrs. Bryce was a longtime resident of Hanover County…"

I switched off the radio and finished the remainder of the drive in glum silence.

Hank Baker, the class instructor and captain of our local search and rescue group, was leaning against his truck when I bounced my SUV across the rutted field and pulled up in front of the barbwire fence where four other vehicles were parked. The others, I was glad to see, had gone ahead without me.

" 'Bout to give up on you," Hank commented as I piled out of the car, dragging my pack behind me. Neither his drawl nor his expression hinted at impatience, but then they never did.

"I'm so sorry," I said, unfastening the dogs' seat belts, "time got away from me. I'm glad you didn't hold up the class. Cisco, release."

Cisco tumbled out of the car with Mischief close on his heels. With no time for niceties, I pushed Mischief back and slammed the door. "Wait," I told her sternly.

The temperature was in the fifties and was likely to remain so until the sun fully cleared the mountains, the front and back windows were open a crack for ventilation, and I wasn't worried about leaving Mischief in the car for an hour or so, particularly since I was surrounded by dog people. Nonetheless, I waited until Mischief settled down in the cargo area and seemed contentedly occupied with her cheese-stuffed bone before I bent to snap on Cisco's tracking lead, apologizing to Hank once again as I did.

"I'm sorry you had to wait for me. I know you're anxious to work your dogs."

"That's okay. I need to let the scent age awhile anyhow." He gestured toward the first of the tiny orange flags. "You're going to be tracking to the west about eight hundred yards, two ninety-degree turns and one false trail. The article is buried in about half an inch of leaf mulch. You okay with that?"

Gamely I nodded, although the truth was that with a dog as erratic as Cisco, to say that I was okay with anything we undertook was always an exercise in optimism. "Good luck, then."

"See you in a bit."

The exercise had been designed so that each tracking team would walk its own course, and the courses were laid out about twenty feet abreast. Typically, we would finish the exercise, which served as more or less of a warm-up for our dogs, in less than half an hour, then reassemble at the cars to discuss what we wanted to practice next. But I should have known that, given the way the day had started, this was not to be a typical morning.

Cisco started out pretty well, nose to the ground, straight tracking, unreeling the cotton tracking lead through my fingers with even, steady pressure. The dew-drenched grass soaked the hem of my jeans, and brambles snatched at my clothes as I trudged along after my dog, my mind only half on the task at hand. I could hear the others in the distance and to the side of me, and I could tell by the direction of their voices that some of them had already finished the exercise and were on their way back.

Abruptly, Cisco lifted his head and sniffed the air. Had my mind been on my work, I would have caught the error before it turned into a full-blown disaster. This was a tracking exercise, after all, and Cisco's nose should have been on the ground. Whatever had distracted him did not belong on this trail. But as it happened I was not watching my dog—a fatal error in search and rescue, and not a particularly smart thing to do at any other time either. I had bent down to pluck up one of the marker flags—it's a simple courtesy to return the flags after we've finished with a course—when suddenly Cisco spun to the left and took off at a gallop.

The last few feet of line flew from my hand. I shouted, "Cisco!" He didn't even look back. I tore off through the brambles after him.

A dog racing through the woods trailing a fifteen-foot line is a disaster waiting to happen. I could only be grateful that the lead was attached to a harness and not his collar; otherwise, he might have snapped his neck. Every once in a while I caught a glimpse of his white tail feathering as he scrambled down a hill or leapt over a fallen log. Once, when the line got caught on a mulberry bush, I got close enough to see what all the fuss was about—a doe and two fawns were racing over a rise a couple of dozen yards away while Cisco strained against his restraint and barked furiously. Of course, as soon as I got close enough to grab the leash, he pulled free and took off again.

A simple rule of thumb: A two-legged human cannot, even under the best of circumstances, hope to catch a four-legged dog. Ever. It's simply not going to happen. I knew this. Nonetheless, I continued to chase. The only reason I eventually caught up with him was that Cisco tired of the sport, lost the trail of the deer and eventually came trotting back, tongue lolling, panting heavily and dragging a line tangled with so many branches and weeds it was a wonder he could drag it at all.

Fortunately for Cisco I was too out of breath to reprimand him and too exhausted to do anything but take a firm hold of his collar and turn him back toward the car. Also fortunately for Cisco, I was a better tracker than he was, or we might have spent the rest of the day wandering around in the woods.

The next to the last car was pulling away from the parking area by the time I limped up, hot, scratched, flushed and furious. A bare arm extended from the window and waved at me, and Hank turned from securing his bloodhound Chloe in her specially built crate attached to the bed of his pickup. He was grinning.

"Wasn't sure whether I should harness up the dogs and send them out after you," he said.

"Deer," I grunted and shrugged out of my pack. Cisco sat obediently at my feet, looking for all the world as though he expected a treat. I scowled at him.

"Yeah, I figured something like that. Fern and Bobby said they saw you tearing out through the woods after him. We didn't feel we had to worry about you finding your way back, so everybody went on home."

I found a bottle of water in my pack and drained half of it. Then, because he was my dog, I poured the rest of the water into a collapsible bowl for Cisco. He lapped it up happily.

I dragged a sleeve across my sweaty face. "He's supposed to be a tracking dog," I grumbled. "A rescue dog, for Pete's sake! With him along, I'm the one who's going to need rescuing. Sometimes I wonder if there's any hope for him at all."

"He's got some spirit, all right," agreed Hank, and tugged affectionately at Cisco's ear. "But he gets the job done when it counts, don't you, fella?"

Cisco licked his hand sloppily. I sighed.

"Sorry I ruined the class." I handed him the flags I had gathered on my way back.

"You didn't ruin anything." He opened the door of his truck and got in. "See you next month, right?"

"Yeah, I'll be there. Next time maybe I'll leave Cisco in the car and put the harness on Mischief."

He grinned and waved, and the truck kicked up a cloud of dust as he drove off.

By this time, it was a quarter till eight, and although Maude knew I had tracking class I still felt bad about being late. "Come on, you scamp," I groused at Cisco, "let's go home."

I put my hand on the rear door latch and said loudly, "Mischief, wait," so that she would not bound out of the vehicle when I swung open the door. At the sound of my voice, Mischief bounced up from the front driver's seat, where she had apparently been enjoying her bone all this time, propped her front paws on the door, and grinned at me through the window. Simultaneously, I heard all four doors lock.

For about two seconds I just stared in outright disbelief. Then I did a frantic, automatic pat down of my pockets, thrust my hands into the pouches of my pack and came up empty on all counts, just as I knew I would. I raced to the driver's door, tugged at it stupidly and saw my keys dangling from the ignition inside. Mischief barked happily.

I leaned against the car door and spent a long time wondering why I had ever gotten into dogs.

I have mentioned that Australian shepherds are fast, dexterous, agile and incredibly clever. They are not, however, clever enough to extract a set of keys from the ignition and drop them through a three-inch crack at the top of the window onto the ground outside. Nonetheless, I actually spent three or four minutes trying to persuade Mischief to do just that, and was rewarded with barks and some new claw marks on the interior of my door as she tried to scratch her way out of the car to me.

Aussies also have excellent hearing. Even inside the closed car, Mischief heard the vehicle coming down the road before either Cisco or I did. She scrambled over the seat and into the back cargo area, ears pricked and eyes sharp, and gave two sharp, staccato barks.

I gathered up Cisco's lead and raced to the road, shouting and waving wildly as a blue Town Car rounded the curve. I didn't recognize the car and at first I thought the driver wouldn't stop. If I had been driving, I'm not sure I would have pulled over for a sweaty, bedraggled, wild-haired woman with a leaping golden retriever on a lead. Well, okay, I might have stopped for the golden retriever.

The car drove on about a hundred yards, pulled over and began to back up. I recognized Dexter Franklin when he lowered the window.

"Hi, Mr. Franklin," I said. "Boy, am I glad to see you! I didn't recognize you without your truck."

"Wife's car," he said shortly. "Damn truck wouldn't start."

His eyes were bloodshot and his face stubbly, and he did not look to be in a good mood. It was not a very well-kept secret that Dexter Franklin liked to hit the bottle now and again, and it looked as though last night had been one of those times. Because he was not a violent drunk and never caused any trouble, most voters in the county chose to see occasional overindulgence as a permissible trait in a commissioner.

Looking me up and down, he said, "You got some kind of trouble?"

I nodded and leaned on the window. "Locked my keys in the car. I don't suppose you..." I brightened as I noticed his toolbox on the floor in the back. "Say, do you have a crowbar?"

He scowled at me. "What the hell has that got to do with anything? No, I don't have a crowbar, and wouldn't let you have it if I did."

I took an involuntary step backward just as he jerked his cell phone from its holder on the dash and thrust it at me. "Here," he said, "call a locksmith. And hurry up. I gotta get to work."

I smiled weakly and took the telephone. "I guess a crowbar was a dumb idea." I also supposed I should be grateful for any help at all, no matter how grudgingly given.

I did not, of course, have the number of the nearest locksmith memorized, so, as much as I hated to, and ever mindful of Dexter Franklin's scowling impatience, I dialed the Hanover County Sheriff's Department.

"Hey, it's Raine," I told the dispatcher. "Listen, I'm stuck here at the southwest entrance to the old Bakersfield farm. You know, right where the power company cut starts off of Highway 6? I accidentally locked my keys in the car. Can you send somebody out here with a jimmy?" She told me it was my lucky day; she had a patrol car about three miles away, and I thanked her and hung up.

"You called the sheriff?" Dexter said as I returned the phone to him. He sounded accusing.

"It's okay," I assured him. "They do this kind of thing all the time." Usually for absentminded little old ladies and damn-fool tourists, of course, and not a grown-up, presumably competent woman like me.

"Well, I don't have time to hang around till they get here." He put the car in gear, and I stepped back quickly, pulling Cisco with me.

"That's okay. Thanks for stopping."

He lifted a dismissive hand as he drove off, and I murmured to his retreating bumper, "You have a good day too." The way the day was going, I should have known that it would be Buck who pulled up a few minutes later. He looked rumpled and exhausted, and if he was still on duty from a shift that should have ended three hours ago, he had every right to be.

"Mischief locked me out," I explained, holding Cisco with both hands to keep him from leaping up on Buck in joy. For Cisco, everything in life was a delightful surprise, and none more treasured than the unexpected presence of his favorite person. I wish I could say I shared his pleasure, but I was embarrassed, disheveled and late, and Buck didn't look any happier about the situation than I was.

He silently took the tool from the trunk of the patrol car, worked it between the door facing and the lock mechanism and popped the lock in about three seconds. I quickly opened the door and snatched the keys from the ignition before Mischief could repeat her trick.

"Thanks," I said, pushing Mischief back into the car. "Sorry to bother you."

"What are you doing out here anyway?"

"Tracking class." I led Cisco around to the back, opened the door and got him quickly into the cargo area, closing the door just before Mischief bounded out. "How'd he do?"

"Great. He tracked a deer for over a mile. Unfortunately, a deer was not what we were supposed to be tracking."

That made him grin, and he plucked a leaf from my hair. "Looks like you've had quite a morning."

"You could say that." I hesitated, watching his expression carefully as I added, "There was a coyote outside the house this morning."

He lifted an eyebrow. "Coyote? Are you sure?"

"Not really. I didn't get much of a look at it.

But it didn't move like a dog."

He returned the tool to the trunk of his squad car and slammed the lid. "Maybe a bobcat."

"Too big." I waited until he looked at me again to add, "Whatever it was set off the security lights. It was inside the fence."

To most people, his expression would have been inscrutable, but not to me. He said carefully, "Doesn't sound like a coyote to me."

"Me either, come to think of it." I watched him. "Anything you want to tell me, Buck?"

"Like?" Nothing in his eyes.

"Like is the FBI watching my house?"

He turned back toward his car. "I'm still on duty, and I've got to get back. You just be careful, you hear?"

"Wait a minute." I scrambled in my backpack for my wallet, opened the change section, and withdrew the necklace I had found at the construction site last night. "If you're going back to the office, will you take this? It belonged to Manny Rodriguez. Maybe someone can see that his family gets it."

Buck looked at the gold necklace as it lay gleaming in my open hand. "Where'd you get that?"

"I found it last night at the construction site. It was beside my tire when I got in to leave. I know it was Manny's because I saw him wearing it yesterday."

Two lines tightened on either side of Buck's mouth, and his lips seemed to lose some color. "You found this last night? When you were leaving?"

I nodded.

"And you've been carrying it around in your pocket all this time?"

"In my purse." I was getting impatient. "And what do you mean, all this time? It's only been a few hours. I was going to go by the office and turn it in this morning, but I'm running late."

"Jesus Christ, Raine!" The outrage in his voice came out like anger. "That's evidence in a federal homicide investigation and you've been carrying it around in your purse?"

"What do you mean, evidence? What do you mean, federal investigation?"

He spun away from me, jerked open the door of the squad car and returned with a small glassine evidence bag. I rolled my eyes. "Oh, come on, Buck; get a grip, will you?"

Tight lipped, he held the bag open before me, and I dropped the necklace into it. I watched while he sealed and labeled the bag.

"Okay, super cop, if you're finished with the dramatics, you want to tell me what this is about?"

"It's about withholding evidence in a homicide investigation. Is that dramatic enough for you?"

I frowned. "I don't see how my finding that necklace a quarter of a mile away from where Manny was killed could have anything to do with a hit-and-run."

He looked at me for a moment, eyes churning with impatience, and seemed to debate whether to say more. Then he said quietly, "Manuel Rodriguez's death is under investigation by the FBI. There's evidence that he might not have been killed on the road at all, but at the construction site. And this"—he held up the evidence bag— "supports that theory."

"What?" I stared at him. "What are you talking about? What has the FBI got to do with this?"

Buck released a short breath. "A known ecoterrorist is in the area. An act of what might very well be ecoterrorism was committed last night and a man was found dead in the vicinity. Why shouldn't the FBI be involved?"

"Oh, for the love of—!" I finished the exclamation with an exasperated toss of my head. "A bear was responsible for your so-called act of ecoterrorism, in case you didn't notice. And last I heard, bears had diplomatic immunity from prosecution."

He regarded me evenly. "A bear didn't slash the tires on those trucks. And a bear didn't take a blunt instrument to Manuel Rodriguez before he ran him over, and then dump his body in a ditch."

For a moment I couldn't speak. "But—why?"

"They think—we think," he corrected himself, "that Rodriguez surprised his killer at the construction site, maybe even tried to stop him from damaging the equipment. He couldn't have any witnesses, so..." He concluded with a lift of his shoulders.

"And you think the killer was Andy?" I was incredulous. "I think that might be one of the first things that pops into any rookie detective's mind," he returned, a little too sharply. He always got snappy when he was defensive. And he was only defensive when he wasn't one hundred percent sure of himself.

"That's crazy!"

"What's crazy about it? It's exactly the kind of cocky thing Andy would do, vandalize the equipment that was tearing up his precious mountains. What better way to thumb his nose at the FBI and let everybody know he's back?"

"Come on, you know better than that! That's exactly the kind of childish, penny ante thing Andy would never do, and he certainly wouldn't kill a man over it!"

"What in the hell makes you think you know what Andy Fontana would or would not do?" Buck demanded. "It's been fifteen years, Raine! The man is a criminal!"

"He did not murder Manny!"

"What makes you so sure of that?"

Because, I thought, if Andy had been at the construction site last night…if he had done the damage to the equipment before the bear arrived…he might have been watching us, watching me, from the woods the whole time. And because suddenly, in the back of my head, I kept hearing that ringtone that had played on my answering machine. "Somewhere Over the Rainbow."

And the last thing I was going to do was tell Buck about that.

I said, "What makes you even think Andy has a car?" He demanded in return, "What makes you think he

doesn't?"

"And I guess next you're going to tell me Andy Fontana charmed the bear and sent him down out of the woods to distract us."

Buck said, "I've got to get back to work."

"Andy didn't do this, Buck. He didn't kill Manny Rodriguez."

He looked at me with his hand on the door handle of his car. His eyes were tired. "You know something, Rainey? Believe it or not, I hope you're right."

He got in the car, but he waited until the dogs and I were securely strapped inside my SUV before he started his engine, and he followed me until I was safely back on the highway.

Thursdays are usually a relatively slow day for us, which is why tracking class on Thursday mornings usually works out well for me. Most of the boarders are dropped off on Friday and picked up on Sunday, and we don't offer any training classes on Thursday. Usually I wouldn't have felt bad about being late, but with the show coming up this weekend, this was no ordinary Thursday.

Although Maude is not as active in breeding and showing golden retrievers in conformation as she once was, she is still very competitive in field trials and obedience with her two champions, River and Rune. River would be competing for the points he needed to earn his Obedience Trial Championship, or OTCH, this weekend, which is the highest honor the AKC obedience community can bestow. Maude had brought River to work with her so that she could put him through his paces in our training room.

Obviously, we couldn't close our kennel for the weekend, even though both of us would be attending the dog show. During the summer, when my part-time work with the forest service kicks in, Mary Ruth Adams comes in to help out on weekends, and she would be minding the store for us while we were away.

Mary Ruth worked part-time for the vet and was very responsible; in many ways she knew the ins and outs of the kennel business as well as we did. Still, Maude had asked her to drop by Thursday morning to go over a few things and to meet the boarders, and while she was doing that someone needed to attend to the office and answer the phone. I had promised I would be back from class in plenty of time to do that.

Needless to say, I did not stop by to work with Mischief in the baseball field. Still, by the time I blew in the door, sputtering apologies and dragging both dogs, Mary Ruth had completed her tour, Maude was finishing up her payroll paperwork and the answering machine was blinking madly.

"I am so sorry," I told Maude after Mary Ruth had gone. Briefly, I explained about the coyote, the deer and Mischief's discovery of automatic door locks. As suited her temperament, she was more amused than annoyed. But her amusement faded when I went on to tell her about Manuel Rodriguez.

"Now Buck is trying to tell me Andy is a suspect in the murder," I told her, sorting through the papers on the desk to find a memo pad. "Have you ever heard anything so silly?"

Her silence made me look up.

"People do change, my dear," she pointed out reasonably. "And you have a tendency to refuse to see the flaws in people you admire."

I scowled. "I don't admire Andy. I just know what he's capable of."

"You must have seen some capability in him that disturbed you all those years ago," she observed, again quite reasonably, "or else you would still be with him."

I couldn't help remembering the cold look in his eyes after the sinking of the freighter, and I shrugged uncomfortably. "Maybe. But I don't think he vandalized that construction site, and I don't think he killed Manuel Rodriguez. It doesn't make sense."

"And I think it's entirely possible that you want to prove Buck wrong on the subject of Andy Fontana once and for all," she replied. "I also think you have enough to worry about right now without telling the police how to do their job. I take it you did not have a chance to work Mischief this morning?"

I sighed. "You take it right. And I think the less I see of that little dog for the rest of the morning the happier we'll both be. Why don't you go ahead and work River, and I'll return some of these phone calls." I sat down behind the desk and pulled a pad and pen toward me. "Maybe after lunch we can take Cisco through his paces. Not," I felt compelled to add, a little sourly, "that it'll do much good at this point."

"Well, that should hardly come as a surprise," returned Maude tartly, "since you've waited until two weeks before the competition to start training him."

"Oh, I beg to differ! I've been training that dog in obedience since he was eight weeks old."

Maude lifted an eyebrow in that perfectly practiced way she has, which managed to rob of any significance whatsoever any argument her opponent might put forth.

Still, I was resolved to give it a try. Scowling, I

pointed out, "He knows everything he needs to know to earn a novice obedience title. You've seen him work. He can perform all of the commands." I was uncomfortably aware that I was starting to sound like one of my own students, full of excuses and justifications for why my dog was not performing at the level I expected him to. I sighed. "Cisco is not an easy dog," I admitted.

"Agreed. All the more reason you need to exercise patience and creativity in his training."

I was starting to get a little worried. "Don't you think he can be ready by the weekend? Should I scratch our entry?"

"Certainly not. You've paid your fee; go out and show your best. I can't help wondering, however," she added, "whether you made the best decision, pulling him out of agility this year."

That was Maude's way of saying, "You bloody idiot, what were you thinking?" though of course she would never say that. Not about my dogs, anyway. What Maude did not understand was the frustration—the heartbreak, really—of training a dog who repeatedly refused to live up to his potential. Especially when there was a lightning-fast Australian shepherd pawing at the gate.

I know it's all supposed to be about the dog. But sometimes you just have to give yourself a treat. And the truth was, Mischief and Magic combined, on their worse day, were easier to train, and far more rewarding, than Cisco on his best.

So I just shrugged and said, "I'm an obedience trainer, for Pete's sake. I should have at least one dog with an obedience title on him. I think it's more important for Cisco to show in obedience than in agility this year, that's all."

"Maybe you should have told Cisco that," suggested Maude mildly, then changed the subject. "What are you going to do about Mischief's weave poles?"

I grimaced. The weave poles are a piece of agility apparatus that requires the dog to weave through six or twelve upright poles, from front to back, without missing a single one. For most dogs, they are the most difficult obstacle, but that was not why I made a face when Maude mentioned them. I still hadn't forgiven Mischief for the mess she had made last night.

"Unless that dog does a lot to endear herself to me between now and Saturday, neither one of us is going to have to worry about her weave poles, because she's going to be sitting in the car during the whole show." I had told Maude about Mischief's adventures in the kitchen last night, and she had found the whole thing terribly amusing.

"Don't be absurd. There hasn't been a car made yet that could hold her. Bring her out as soon as you finish there and we'll work her weave poles before it gets too hot."

Maude added, "River, heel," in a perfectly conversational tone, and a magnificent golden retriever sprang up from the dog bed upon which he had been curled and trotted to perfect heel position at her side. I felt a pang of admiration, liberally laced with envy, just to watch him. River was actually a distant cousin of Cisco's—both of them could trace their ancestry back to the mother of my wonderful Cassidy, who had belonged to Maude—and I had hopes that I too might one day achieve that kind of flawless obedience from

Cisco.

At this point, however, that day seemed to be in the very, very distant future.

River stepped when she stepped, and Maude did not give another command as the two of them left the room in perfect unison. I sighed, watching them, then turned to the answering machine and punched up the first message.

There were a couple of requests for boarding reservations, and one inquiry about obedience classes, and the fourth or fifth call was a familiar, vacant-sounding voice.

"Miss Stockton, this is Olivia Foster. I just wanted you to know we won't be there for class next week, since Baby Face got eaten by that bear last night. You said we were supposed to call if we weren't going to be there. Bye, now."

I stared at the machine. I punched replay. The message did not change, and I hadn't misheard it. I scrambled through the file cabinet for my class list, found Mrs. Foster's telephone number and dialed it. She answered on the fourth ring.

"Mrs. Foster?" I said. "This is Raine Stockton. You know, from dog class."

She said, "Oh."

"I just got your message, about Baby Face."

"Oh," she replied. "Yes. He got eaten by that bear, you know."

I swallowed hard. "I'm so sorry. But—are you sure? I mean, maybe he just got lost or something."

"No," she replied complacently, "he's not lost. Henry buried him this morning."

"Oh." Not much to say to that, except to repeat, "I'm so sorry."

"Okay."

Sensing she was about to hang up, I interjected quickly, "Mrs. Foster—bears don't usually eat dogs, you know. I wonder if it's possible that, well, that something else might have happened to Baby Face?"

"Oh, I don't think so. I saw it myself. Thank you for calling. Good-bye."

And I found myself listening to a dial tone.

I went to find Maude.

She was not in the air-conditioned training room, and I was about to check the kennels when I saw her through the window, standing outside the play yard talking with a young man I did not recognize. To my amazement, her usually perfectly behaved River, who was inside the play yard, was leaping and flinging himself at the fence, tongue lolling, barking shamelessly. When Maude turned and raised a silencing finger at him, he stopped barking but continued to leap and grin and throw himself at the fence.

That, of course, was when I realized that the beautifully behaved River was actually lying quietly at Maude's feet, and the wild creature who was trying to escape the play yard was my own Cisco. The young man to whom Maude was talking, most likely a potential client, was beginning to cast uneasy glances toward the crazed golden retriever who was exhibiting an ecstasy of overly enthusiastic greeting behavior.

Humiliated and annoyed, I strode outside, crossed the yard and slammed open the gate of the play yard. Cisco saw me coming and he knew I wasn't happy. He sat down, licked his lips nervously and then gave me his most endearing, panting grin.

I wasn't buying it. I snapped on his leash, gave him a curt "Heel!" command and marched him out of the play yard.

Maude and the stranger were only about twenty feet from the play yard, but it took Cisco and me almost a minute to reach them, because every time Cisco started to break heel position, I stopped forward motion and made him sit and wait. If he had any hope at all of earning a passing score at the obedience trial this weekend, he had to understand what the word "heel" meant. After all, my reputation as a dog trainer was at stake, and Cisco was becoming more of a liability than an advertisement for my business.

When we reached Maude, I put Cisco, who was by now beginning to figure out that I was in no mood to be trifled with, in a perfect sit at my side, where he continued to shuffle uneasily and make soft, almost indiscernible whining noises. It was then that I noticed that he didn't seem to be nearly as interested in the stranger as he was in something behind him. And the only thing behind Maude and the newcomer was woods.

I extended my hand to the stranger. "Hi, I'm Raine Stockton. I apologize for all the noise a minute ago. My dogs are usually better behaved."

Maude, also obviously eager to excuse my ill-mannered canine, said, "I think he may have seen a deer, Raine. He was perfectly fine in the play yard, and then he became awfully agitated, as though he wanted to get out and chase something."

"There was something lurking around the house this morning," I admitted uneasily and tried not to peer too obviously into the woods beyond the stranger's shoulder.

"Maybe it was a bear," suggested the man.

I gave him a patronizing smile. "That's not very likely, with all these dogs around. Are you here about a dog?"

"Actually, no," he said. "I'm here about a bear."

My confusion—it was probably more like shock— must have registered in my face, because Maude interjected quickly, "Raine, this is Marcus Hanes. He's the new reporter at the paper."

"Oh," I said, trying to remember whether I was supposed to know this or not, and if I was, why it should matter. The newspaper hired a new reporter approximately every three months, since it took that long for a young person to figure out that the glamour of being a feature reporter did not offset the fact that one couldn't possibly make a living on what the job paid.

Cisco, sensing my lack of attention, tried to sneak in a quick, bouncing leap toward the woods. I tightened the leash with a snap and scowled at him. To the reporter I said, "Well, I don't know how you got hold of this story, but I can assure you that a bear did not eat Olivia Foster's dog." Maude turned a startled gaze on me, but I plunged on. "Black bears are opportunists. They don't come down out of the mountains looking to kill and eat, and they only attack in self-defense or in defense of their young. The only possible scenario I can picture is that the puppy tried to chase the bear and got swatted or stepped on. But please don't let Mrs. Foster tell you that a bear made dinner out of her pet. That's only going to start a panic. Even if the bear were wounded or sick—"

He looked up from his furious scribbling. "Like with rabies?"

"Rabies?" I was appalled. "Who told you that?"

"Bears can get rabies, can't they?"

"All mammals can get rabies. But I really don't think—"

"Isn't unusual behavior one of the symptoms of rabies in wild animals? You know, like showing no fear of people, coming out in the open in the bright daylight, that kind of thing?"

"Well," I admitted, "it can be. But those can also be symptoms of distemper, or almost anything that affects the neurological system."

Maude said meaningfully, "Of course I'm sure Raine wouldn't want to be quoted on that. She's not a veterinarian."

I gave Maude a grateful look, and Marcus still scribbling, murmured, "Right. I'll give Doc Withers a call." Ken Withers was our local vet.

"Actually," he went on, "I came out here to ask you about the bear at the construction site last night. One of the workers got some pretty good pictures of it, and the sheriffs department said you were the wildlife specialist on the scene. Now would this be the same bear that ate"—he glanced at his notes—"Mrs. Foster's pet? How big was the dog, do you know?"

I glanced helplessly at Maude and knew I was in deep trouble. I spent the next half hour trying to undo the damage, but to no avail.

The next morning the headline of our weekly paper read: *Rabid bear ravages county.*

On page two, midway down, was a column headed: *Man killed in hit-and-run*. Manuel Rodriguez didn't even rate a photograph.

Chapter Eight

"So I guess I'm fired, huh?" I said glumly to Rick the next day.

He gave me a glare that would have sent most people slinking for the door. "If I thought firing you would fix this, you'd be out of here in a heartbeat."

I knew Rick well enough to wait until the harsh lines faded from his face, which they did in about ten seconds. He sighed and added, "If anyone needs to be fired, it's that kid at the Chronicle. I've already spoken to Ed." Ed Slocum was the publisher and editor of the newspaper. "He says he'll print a correction next week, for all the good it will do. Said he would've checked out the facts with me first, but—"

"But the reporter had already checked them out with me," I finished for him.

"Yeah."

The silence in the small cabin was as heavy as the gray day that pushed against its walls.

"At least I found out what really happened to Mrs. Foster's dog," I offered in a moment. "The dog next door is a Rottweiler-pit bull mix. Its name is Bear."

A look of distaste mixed with incredulity crossed his face. "And it...?"

I nodded sadly. "Neither Mrs. Foster nor the neighbors keep their dogs leashed. The little Jack Russell wandered into the bigger dog's territory, they got into a scrap, and...well."

He shook his head. "Bear. Of all the damned-fool things. I mean, it's a shame and all, but—"

"Yes, it is a shame," I agreed rather sharply. "It wasn't the puppy's fault. It wasn't even Bear's fault. They were both just being dogs. It's the owners who are to blame. Next time it could be a child."

I could tell Rick thought I was trying to change the subject and deflect the blame, although one would think that by now he would know that for me dogs are always the subject. Still, I gave an apologetic shrug and added, "I'll make sure the paper prints that story next week, right beside their correction about bears and rabies."

Rick said somberly, "You know what we're going to have to do, don't you?"

I was shaking my head before he even finished speaking. "Come on, Rick, let's not overreact. It's a stupid newspaper story. Everybody knows not to believe half of what they read in that rag—"

"It's not just the story. We had three sightings last week, not to mention the half dozen complaints about screens torn off porches, trash cans raided—"

"Excuse me, these people are living in the middle of a national forest! What do they expect? We're the ones who invaded the bears' territory, not the other way around. If Ed Slocum wants a story for his paper, that's the one he ought to print!"

"Be that as it may, we're moving into tourist season and these woods are going to be full of campers and kayakers and hikers. If we've got a bear who's a known nuisance and there should happen to be an incident..."

"There's not going to be an incident," I insisted. "We have bears come down out of the woods every year. If people would just let them be—"

"Somebody is going to shoot him," Rick said flatly, "if we don't tranquilize and relocate him."

I knew he was right. But I also knew that if we relocated the bear out of his own familiar territory, his chances of survival would be decreased dramatically— not to mention the damage that could be done to the ecology of the new environment when an unfamiliar predator was introduced. There was nothing good about that solution, and the thought that I could be responsible for it made me feel ill.

I said suddenly, "What if I can prove he's innocent?"

Rick sat back in his chair, a flash of amusement in his face. "What?"

"I mean, so far all we've had are two real incidents, right? That construction worker's truck, and the Tuckers' workshop."

"Three," corrected Rick. "Dave Runsford saw him tramping through his blueberry bushes."

I waved a dismissing hand. "So, what are a few blueberry bushes? And all he did at the Tuckers' was spill a little birdseed."

"Well, he did a lot more damage at the construction site than just that one truck. Besides, it's not a matter of degree; it's a matter of frequency."

"That's exactly what I mean. It's not just one incident that makes a bear a nuisance. There has to be a pattern that shows he sees people as a source of food. So, what if there isn't a pattern? All those other things—the trashcans, the torn screens— they could have been done by vandals, or kids playing pranks. As for the construction site, all we really know is that a bear got stuck in a pickup truck because the owner left the windows down and a bunch of food inside. It might not even be the same bear."

Rick looked at me skeptically for a moment, then said, "You do what you have to, Raine. But the next time I get a call about a bear, I've got to go out with the tranq gun."

"Well, I just hope he has sense enough to stay holed up in the woods, then."

"Believe it or not," replied Rick, "so do I."

The phone started to ring, and Rick put his hand on the receiver. "Are we done here?"

"Yeah." I stood. "Now I've got to go get yelled at by my uncle."

"Your uncle? What did you to do him?"

I nodded toward the ringing phone. "The sheriff's department gets the bear calls first."

"I'll see you Monday, Raine."

"Thanks, Rick."

I closed the screen door gently behind me just as he was saying, "Ranger station."

Gray-white scraps of cloud were draped like tattered gauze curtains over the mountains when I came out, and the first few fat drops of rain had left blotches of clean on my dusty vehicle. We needed the rain badly, but I found myself hoping that if this front was settling in to stay, it wouldn't extend as far as Asheville for the weekend. There is nothing more disheartening than trying to hold a dog show in the rain.

However, by the time I made my way down the mountain and into town, the clouds had dissipated into the famous curls of "smoke" that give our mountains their name, and it was beginning to look as though the most we could expect out of them was a layer of humidity just thick enough to make the day miserable.

I parked in the visitors' lot of the Public Safety Building, which seemed to be unusually crowded, and made my way inside.

The sheriff's office and jail were housed in a relatively new complex that was designed to be "grown into" and was, under normal circumstances, more than big enough to accommodate its occupants. These were apparently anything but normal circumstances, because when I entered the building I barely recognized the place.

The muted cacophony of many voices, the ringing of many telephones and the presence of many bodies—most of them unfamiliar to me—were the first things I noticed. The next thing I noticed was Deke Williams, one of Uncle Roe's deputies, standing guard just inside the door with his hands resting lightly on his gun belt. Perhaps this should have been the first thing I noticed, because when I started to move past him, he stepped in front of me, blocking my way.

"Sorry, Miz Lawson," he said. "I can't let you in without ID."

Some people, especially people who were friends of Buck's before they were friends of mine, still insist upon calling me by my married name. Most of them don't do it for long if they care to stay friends with either Buck or me, but Deke Williams was one of those people who just didn't seem to be able to catch on to that fact. Likewise, it seemed futile to point out that, since he had just called me by name, asking for ID was a bit redundant.

I dug in my back pocket for my driver's license, peeled away the ten dollar bill and the plastic dog-waste bag that were wrapped around it—I never travel without one— and plopped the license in his hand. No doubt he noticed that the name on the license was Raine Stockton, because he peered at me suspiciously, checked the photo again and said, "You need to get your name changed on your license."

I snatched the piece of plastic away from him. "What the hell is going on here, Deke?"

He said, "Are you carrying any weapons, cameras, or cell phones?"

I flung my arms out to the side, planted my feet and demanded, "Do I look like I am?" I was wearing skintight jeans, a T-shirt that actually fit, and sandals. Where would I have hidden any of the items he mentioned?

Deke looked uncomfortable, glanced around and said, "We've got to search you, Miz Lawson."

I was out of patience. "I'd check my insurance policy before I did that if I were you, Deke, because I never heard of a surer way to lose your front teeth. Now, get out of my way. My uncle is expecting me."

He looked as though he would try to give me an argument, but then an unfamiliar voice said, "I'll vouch for this woman, Deputy," and he stepped back.

I turned and tried not to scowl at my rescuer. "Well, Special Agent Dickerson, as I live and breathe. I guess we have you to thank for all this?" I gestured to include the guard at the door, the makeshift desks and computers that were set up in every possible corner and the telephone lines and cables that snaked across the linoleum and around the baseboards.

As I spoke I walked, and he fell into step beside me. I got the distinct impression I was being escorted.

"It seemed more efficient to set up a temporary task force here, since we're working so closely with the local authorities."

The front desk receptionist gave me a harried look as I passed by and I returned a sympathetic one. Two men in sports jackets I didn't know walked past me, their heads bent over a file. They were wearing shoulder holsters. No one wore shoulder holsters around here. No one around here walked past you without speaking, for that matter. I hated this.

I said, "And this is how you plan to keep your little manhunt a secret? Good luck with that."

I actually thought he smiled. "We do have a cover story."

"Oh? What's that?"

"Disaster drill."

I shot him a skeptical, sideways look. "Are you sure you people are from the FBI?"

We had reached my uncle's door, which was

closed for what I believed to be the first time since he had taken office more than twenty years ago. The sight of it gave me a chill.

Special Agent Dickerson tapped lightly on the door and, without waiting for a reply, opened it a fraction. In a moment he opened it even wider and another unfamiliar man came out. This one at least nodded at me but seemed far too busy to meet my eyes.

I went inside my uncle's cramped office and Dickerson pulled the door closed behind me. Deliberately, I opened it again and left it open as he walked away.

When most people looked at Uncle Roe they thought round. It wasn't that he was fat; in fact, he was in pretty good shape for a man his age whose only exercise was walking from his car to his desk. But he was on the short side, with a balding head and a pleasant, unassuming expression, and when you looked at him you thought: gentle, harmless, round. For the most part, that was exactly what he was.

He had shot a man in the line of duty once. A mean drunk had just beaten his wife half to death and fired three shots into a patrol car, striking a deputy. Uncle Roe had taken careful aim and shot the man to death. People still talked about that incident, but Uncle Roe never did.

He turned from the filing cabinet, gave me a measured look and gestured for me to sit down. Lines of fatigue made his face look more angular than round. Still, he was my uncle, so I crossed the room and hugged him. "How long has it been since you slept?" I demanded.

"Don't try to get on my good side, Rainbow,"

he answered gruffly, hugging me back. "Do you have any idea how much trouble you've caused?"

"Did you eat breakfast this morning? Do you want me to run get you a sausage biscuit?"

He scowled. "Do you really think your aunt Mart would let me out of the house without breakfast? Sit down."

I took the hard, straight-backed visitor's chair in front of his desk, and he leaned back in his desk chair, his arms folded across his chest. "Did you ever see such a zoo?'

"No," I admitted. "And I should know from zoos." That almost made him smile.

"I'm sorry about the mix-up with the paper, Uncle Roe. I know you've got enough to do without chasing all over the county following bogus bear sightings. Rick already chewed me out."

He hesitated, then sighed. "Matter of fact, you probably did us a favor. As long as the paper is chasing after bear stories, they don't have time to be chasing after us. And it would be hard to ignore what's been going on around here the past couple of days."

"Do you really think anybody's going to buy that phony disaster drill story?"

"Well, it's got a little more bite to it than that. What they're actually letting out is that they're practicing for a terrorist attack on the Cullowhee Gorge Bridge. Since something like that would cut off one of the major arteries to Asheville, it's not all that far-fetched."

I was horrified. "They're not really going to close down the road to Asheville, are they?" Just to show how my mind works, all I could think about was how I was going to get to the dog show tomorrow.

"Nah. I think they're planning to leak the story to the radio Monday, and by the time the paper picks it up, this whole thing should be over."

I actually drew a breath to inquire how he could possibly know that, but even as I did a closed expression came over his face and I saw him lift one cautionary finger from his chest. Police business. More important, FBI business, and he would answer no more questions.

I said, "Actually, the reason I came by— besides the bear, that is—was to ask you about that fellow who was killed in the hit-and-run, Manuel Rodriguez. I knew him."

Uncle Roe's face doesn't show surprise easily, and he showed none now. But he did lean forward and fold his hands on his desk. "You knew him? How?"

"I guess I should have said I met him once. He came over to pet Cisco while I was in the Feed and Seed. He said he had a dog like him at home."

Roe nodded, understanding. I met all kinds of people through my dogs. "Buck didn't mention that. He did say you kept a piece of evidence overnight in your purse. And you a judge's daughter."

I bristled despite the fact that there was absolutely no note of accusation in Uncle Roe's tone or eyes.

"How was I supposed to know it was evidence? I didn't even know he was dead when I found the necklace. All I was trying to do is return a piece of lost jewelry to its owner."

He said, "I explained that to the FBI."

"Do you really think he was killed there at the site—I mean, that it wasn't just an accidental hit-and-run?"

He hesitated, as though trying to decide how much was public record and how much was official business. We usually weren't so careful with each other. "There's evidence of a struggle. Looks like Rodriguez was struck with something—maybe a hammer or crowbar the perpetrator used to damage some of the equipment. He staggered off, made it to the road and was struck from behind. That's what killed him."

"So there could have been two people involved?" I asked. "The one who fought with him and the one in the car?"

But Uncle Roe was already shaking his head. "Not likely. The tire tracks show a vehicle coming down the road from the construction site actually swerve off the road to strike Rodriguez, then swerve back onto the blacktop. Unfortunately, that's all they show. Not very easy to isolate tire tracks at a construction site."

I tried to imagine the deliberate viciousness behind such a crime. It was hard enough to think of someone striking a person with his car and just driving off, bur to deliberately swerve off the road to hit him. "What kind of person would do that?" I wondered out loud.

Uncle Roe just gazed at me, and I thought I saw a trace of pity far back in his eyes. Maybe I imagined it.

I said, "The FBI is looking at the wrong man for this one, Uncle Roe."

He replied, after a long and heavy silence.

"Just be careful for a while, okay, Rainbow?"

My mouth went a little dry, and I knew he was not talking about the investigation into a simple hit-and-run. But I managed a smile. "I talked to Aunt Mart last night. I told her I can't make it to Sunday dinner. I've got a dog show this weekend."

"Too bad. But I'm going to be busy down here, so probably better to make it another day."

"Yeah, that's what she thought."

"Well, bring home some ribbons."

"You bet."

Chapter Nine

I saw Buck's car parked in front of Miss Meg's Cafe, and I pulled into the spot that had just been vacated beside it. He often stopped there for breakfast after his shift, and there were a couple of things I wanted to talk to him about.

That wasn't the only reason I stopped. I remembered that the construction workers liked to eat here, which was why I had missed out on lunch the last time I was in town. And as luck would have it, two of the men who had been at the construction site the night of the bear mischief were just coming out of the door as I got out of my car.

I called, "Hi!" and waved as they looked around. "I'm Raine Stockton," I reminded them as I approached. "From the other night? With the bear?"

They seemed to recognize me and waited until I reached them. The fellow whose truck had been destroyed wasn't with them, so I asked, "How's your friend's truck?"

"Insurance'll cover it," replied one of the men. "We got pictures."

"So I noticed. I saw some of them in the paper."

"Say, do bears really get rabies?" asked the other man, and I had to spend a few minutes explaining that the bear did not have rabies, that he was only exhibiting a perfectly natural foraging instinct and that bears were usually very shy creatures and I doubted they would see him again.

"Anyway, old Micky had enough and quit. He called his brother to come get him and went on back to South Carolina."

"Gee, that's too bad. That means you've lost two men this week."

Both of them looked blank until I reminded them, "Manny Rodriguez. The man who was killed?"

"Oh, the Mexican. Yeah, that was something, all right. But he didn't really work with us. Those boys were mostly on the brush crew—you know, clearing out brush where it's too soft for the dozers to go, minding the fires, that sort of thing. I mean, don't none of us speak Spanish."

"We liked him okay," the other man put in, tapping out a cigarette. "Like all of them, they're pretty good old boys. Just don't hang around much, you know. Sometimes they ride back to the hotel with us after supper. Matter of fact, that Manny, he was supposed to meet us at the site after supper for a ride that night the bear tore everything up. He never showed. With all the excitement, we never thought no more about it and then the next thing we know the sheriff's department's back up there asking all kinds of questions and we hear he was killed." He shook his head and lit the cigarette. "Damn shame."

"Hell, I knew somebody was going to get killed on that road," pointed out the other man. "The way people drive around here—"

"We was almost run off the road the other night, remember, Duke? Some half-drunk idiot in a pickup come flying around the curve about eighty miles an hour, not caring a thing in this world about who else was on the road—"

"It was bound to happen, all right," agreed Duke. "But a damn shame."

Apparently whoever had interviewed them had not mentioned that the hit-and-run was not an accident. I said, "Did Manny get along pretty well with everybody? I mean, was there ever any trouble or anything?"

The men shared a glance. "That sheriff's deputy asked us the same thing. Y'all ain't thinking somebody run him over on purpose, are you?"

"I think they're looking at all angles," I hedged and was glad Buck had introduced me the other night as "Officer Stockton." If they thought I had some official connection to this investigation, I wasn't about to disillusion them.

Duke lifted a shoulder. "Some of the boys don't like working with Mexicans, and that's a fact. Told the deputy the same thing. But they're all talk. You know how it is. Me, I figure as long as a man does his job, I got no beef with where he comes from."

"What about Micky?" I asked, trying to sound casual. "Did he feel the same way?"

Duke ground out his cigarette, and I couldn't

help noticing that he didn't meet my eyes. "I reckon. Never talked about it. Guess we'd better get going."

"Hey, Raine."

I looked over my shoulder to greet Meg, who had just stepped out front to light a cigarette. There are probably more people who still smoke in North Carolina than in any other state in the union, and when you realize that for most of its existence North Carolina has supported itself on tobacco revenue, it's not hard to understand why. Meg was long past her prime, and the smoker's lines around her mouth and eyes made her look even older, but cigarettes were a habit she declared over and over she had no intention of quitting.

I greeted her, and Meg acknowledged the two men, who had apparently become regulars, with a friendly, "How ya doin', fellas? Your breakfast okay?"

"Just fine, Miss Meg. What kind of pie are you having for lunch?"

"You just come on back and see. I declare I don't know what to do with a bunch of men that ain't got nothing better to do than hang around outside a diner and wait for their next meal." But she said it in such an easy, teasing way that both men grinned. "Y'all get on back in your truck now and free up that parking space for somebody else. And try to find some useful work, why don't you?"

"Well, I tell you the truth, I wouldn't mind that myself," said one as he opened the driver's door. "We're on half wages till we get that equipment up and running again, and I didn't come all the way from South Carolina to sit around and watch soap operas in a hotel room, I'll tell you that."

"Now you're just breaking my heart. I might have to save you boys an extra piece of my pecan pie for lunch." They grinned and waved to her as they drove off, and I said, "Well, it's easy to see why the diner is the most popular eating place in town."

"My pie?"

"You. You make everybody feel like they're eating at home."

She shrugged, looking a little embarrassed, and took another drag on the cigarette. "Well, nice don't cost nothing, and a girl's got to make a living. Besides, these boys are a long way from home; they need somebody to talk to."

"I hate to say it, but I don't think everybody in town is feeling quite as cordial toward them as you are."

"Well, if they own a business they ought to be. Money is money; I don't care whose pocket it comes out of."

I laughed. "You're a card, Meg. You talk like the only reason you're in this business is to make money, when I know perfectly well it's because you just plain like people."

She lifted one shoulder in another half shrug. "Well, it gives a body something to do. Were you talking to them about that poor Mexican boy that got himself killed?"

I nodded, unsurprised that Meg had picked up the gist of the conversation. She knew everything.

"What a shame that was, and him just the sweetest thing." She drew on her cigarette. "Always left a tip even though he couldn't have been making more than a couple of dollars an hour, and put on a clean shirt before he came in too, which is more than I can say for some people. That's why it made me so mad when that one fellow started talking that way about him, trying to cause trouble."

"What fellow?" I said quickly.

"I don't know his name. Little bandy-legged fellow, used to come in with those two." She jerked her head toward the place where the two construction workers had parked their truck. "Had a mouth on him, is all I know. Always making these little digs about the Mexican fellow, knowing he didn't hardly speak English. Seemed right cowardly to me. Then the other night he went too far, said something about it being a relief for white people not having to sit at the same table as a wetback, started telling some ugly joke about a senorita, and I just marched right up to him and said that if he couldn't keep a civil tongue in his head he didn't ever have to come back to my establishment, and," she concluded with a smoky exhalation of satisfaction, "he ain't been back since."

"What night was that?" I asked.

"Wednesday. Catfish special."

The night Manny was killed. "And Manny didn't come in that night?"

"Awful to think he was lying dead in that ditch the whole time. Probably got hit on his way down here to get some supper."

"He didn't usually ride in with the other guys?"

"Honey," she pointed out patiently, "they didn't associate, not at suppertime anyway."

"But those guys just said they all used to ride back to the hotel together."

"I'm not saying they didn't. But the Mexicans always came in about five o'clock, and most of them was cleared out by the time the white boys came in at six. That's why it galled me so when that big mouth started making comments about having to eat with them, when there wasn't hardly ever any overlap between them."

The bell over the diner door jangled as Buck came out. "Mornin', ladies," he said. "Fine meal, Meg."

"Well, I guess I better get back to it," she said, patting Buck's arm by way of greeting. "Y'all take care, now, you hear?"

"Thanks, Meg," I murmured.

I must have been frowning in my confusion because as she went inside, Buck said, "Those guys weren't giving you a hard time, were they?"

"What? Who?" Then I shook my head, realizing he must have seen me talking to the construction workers from the window. "Oh, them. They're okay. No, they just wanted to know if bears really get rabies."

He chuckled, chewing on a toothpick as we walked toward our cars. "You sure made a mess of that one, Rainbow Rabbit, if you don't mind my saying so."

"Don't call me that!" I snapped, and he lifted an eyebrow.

"Touchy today, aren't we?"

"Well, if you'd had a morning like I have, you would be too. First I had to get raked over the coals by Rick, then I had to be practically strip-searched before I could get in to see my own uncle, and why can't Deke ever remember my name, anyway?"

"Yeah, well, I wouldn't know anything about having bad days, sweetheart. All I ever do is sit around and eat donuts."

I noticed the exhaustion in his face, the rumpled uniform and the stubble of beard with a stab of guilt. "Are you just now getting off? I thought you were working seven to seven."

"I am. Except for this week, and next week and maybe the week after." He yawned. "As long as it takes."

"Looks like with half the Raleigh bureau down here you guys would get a little bit of a break."

"Well, maybe we would," he agreed, cutting his eyes to me, "if we didn't have to go running down every damn-fool account of a rabid bear that got called in."

I grimaced. "All right, I get it already." I changed the subject quickly as we reached my car. "Are you going to be able to get up in time to watch Cisco compete in the morning?"

Buck was Cisco's biggest fan. Since he was the one who had gone to the trouble of tracking down one of the last litters directly descended from Cassidy, and had gone all the way to Ohio to pick up Cisco and then had presented him to me as a gift shortly after Cassidy died, the attachment was only natural, I suppose. Except for an official emergency or two, Buck hadn't missed a single competition in Cisco's career, and he always reserved the time off well in advance of a show. But the look on his face told me there was a first time for everything.

"Oh, Buck, you didn't forget? This is the

biggest show of the year!"

He was already shaking his head. "I told you, all leaves are canceled. Nobody's getting off this weekend. Damn, I'm sorry. Are you showing him in agility?"

"No, obedience."

He chuckled. "Now, I do wish I could be there to see that. Good luck."

"Yeah, thanks. I know I'm going to need it." I walked around the back of my car toward the driver's door, and Buck started toward his own vehicle. Suddenly he stopped.

"Where did you get that?" he said.

It took me a moment to figure out what he was staring at. I do have a few bumper stickers on my car: MY GOLDEN RETRIEVER IS SMARTER THAN YOUR HONOR STUDENT; LORD, MAKE ME THE KIND OF PERSON MY DOG THINKS I AM; and—my favorite—IF YOU THINK IT'S HARD TO PUT A CONDOM ON IN THE DARK, TRY DOING IT WITH PAWS, SPAY OR NEUTER YOUR PET! But none of those had caused the sudden look of consternation on Buck's face.

There was a brand new bumper sticker on my car, all shiny and colorful next to the dirty, banged-up ones that surrounded it. It was a rainbow. That was all. *Just a rainbow.*

Buck looked at me sharply. "Raine? Where did you get that?"

The first love note Andy had ever sent me was after a fight we had about something stupid— probably about him driving me crazy singing that silly song—and it had said simply "I" with a drawing of a heart and a drawing of a rainbow. *I Heart Rainbow.* I had fallen into his arms and we had made passionate love, and after that I would find those little drawings everywhere: in the steam of the bathroom mirror, in my sock drawer, on the bottom of the grocery list, in the dust on my car. He never signed a note to me, not even one that said "Gone jogging," without leaving that drawing. I Heart Rainbow.

But Buck didn't know that. How could Buck know that?

Had I told him?

He said again, "Raine?" before I could get my voice back, and then I had to clear my throat.

"I—um, someone put it there. Gave it to me, I mean. One of the kids, maybe, from obedience class."

As I tried to move past him, he actually grabbed my arm. I jerked away. "What's the matter with you? It's a stupid nickname. Why shouldn't I have a bumper sticker?"

Buck's face had taken on the tinge of the leaden day. He said, "It's also the symbol of the People for a Clean Planet."

The inside of my throat felt like corrugated steel. I couldn't swallow. But somehow I managed to jerk my chin up defiantly and reply, "Also the symbol for the Rainbow Coalition, the gay rights movement, and lots of other things—including my name!"

He stood right in front of me, so close that I could smell the stale, used odor of his clothes, the hint of leather that clung to them from the police car, the coffee on his breath. They were good scents, familiar scents, and they had always meant safety to me. But when he looked at me, I was afraid.

"That was no coyote you saw yesterday

morning," he said.

And I answered, "The only coyotes I've seen lately are the ones you've taken up with."

"When has your car been out of your sight?"

"I'm not doing this, Buck."

"We could impound your car."

"You're not doing any such goddamned thing!" My voice had risen to a pitch that was causing the diners who were entering and leaving the cafe to glance our way, but I didn't care. I could feel myself starting to shake, and I knew I had to get away from him. "It's a twenty-five-cent bumper sticker that you can pick up in half the stores in this town and it's not against the law to have it on my car, so I'm going home."

This time I pushed past him, and somewhat to my surprise, he let me. I fumbled open the door, then turned back to him. "By the way," I said, "if you and the FBI would spend a little more time interviewing real suspects instead of chasing rainbows"—I spat out the word—"you might not have let that Micky person leave the state. A bear can do a lot of damage to a truck, but it can disguise a lot more."

He stepped aside to allow me to back out of the parking place, and I did not look behind me as I drove off.

Chapter Ten

One of the good things about owning your own business is that, for the most part and within reason, you can set your own hours. During the competitive dog show season, we made sure all our clients knew that we closed at noon on Fridays. There was therefore always a big rush to pick up and drop off dogs before lunchtime on Fridays, and I had left Maude to handle it alone.

I got back home a little after ten, and for the next forty-five minutes I was too busy to even apologize to Maude. Amazingly, at eleven o'clock, she closed the door behind the last client, turned the lock, flipped the closed sign and declared, "That's it. Annabelle Lee was the last drop off, and the Porters called this morning to say they won't be picking up Dude until Monday. We're finished."

I tapped the last entry into the computer and sat back in the desk chair, waving a hand at her. "Go," I said. "I'll finish up."

"I do believe I'll take you up on that." She plucked her rain jacket from the coat rack, although it was clear by now that any possibility of rain was long gone. "I won't even ask how your interview with Rick went because I can guess. What time are you leaving in the morning?"

"Five," I said. "That should give me half an hour to get the dogs settled in before Cisco shows. I can set up after the group exercises."

"Very good. I'll look for you after I set up. Drive safely."

One might think it would make sense for the two of us to travel together, since we were both going to the same place at the same time. But with four dogs and all the equipment that entailed— including four crates, two shade canopies, a cooler containing people food, dog treats and enough soft drinks and water to last everyone concerned all day, not to mention several bags of miscellaneous necessities—there simply wasn't room in one vehicle. This was also why we took half days off on Fridays before a show. It could take literally half a day to pack the car.

As soon as dust from the drive obscured Maude's car, I abandoned the computer, left the kennels to be checked later and locked up the office. I went immediately to my car, but not to pack it with show supplies. I dragged out the hose, a bucket of soapy water and a stiff brush and began to scrub the bumper sticker off my car.

My throat felt as gluey as the stubborn paper I was trying to remove, and I kept remembering the look on Buck's face. When had my car been out of my sight? When was the last time I had looked at the back bumper?

I parked every night on the side of the house closest to the kennel, less than fifty feet from the wood line.

My car had also been out in the open, practically abandoned, behind the ranger station in the middle of the national forest for more than an hour twice this week.

But why would anyone take that kind of chance to leave a bumper sticker on my car? It was just stupid.

Why would anyone leave a ringtone message on my answering machine?

For that matter, if a person was a fugitive from the law and the county was swarming with FBI agents, where would he even get a cell phone with fancy ringtones? Much less a rainbow bumper sticker. Why would he take a chance on acquiring two such basically useless items—useless, at least, for someone who could easily live off the land for years without ever venturing close to civilization—and why would he risk everything to contact me?

Just to prove he could?

I got most of the sticky paper off and decided as long as I had the hose out I might as well give the SUV a long-overdue bath. Later, Cisco and Mischief would be given the same treatment, only with pleasant-smelling shampoo in our grooming room. A lot of people thought it was a waste of time to groom a dog who wasn't showing in conformation, especially since they would only end up filthy by the end of the day, but I never took my dogs out in public looking anything other than their shiny-coated, bright-eyed best.

I was just rolling up the hose again when I caught sight of a familiar car turning into my driveway. Every muscle in my body tensed.

Buck lives less than five miles from me, in the house he grew up in and took over from his mother when she moved to Florida. Sometimes he stops by on his way to town to see if I need anything, or on his day off to bring me supper. He's good about checking on the dogs if I'm late getting in from somewhere, or if I have to be gone overnight. But he doesn't make a pest of himself. And he hardly ever just stops by in the middle of the day after he's worked a fourteen-hour shift.

He pulled in behind me and got out of the car, avoiding the mud puddle the hose had left. He had showered and changed into cutoff shorts and a clean T-shirt, and sneakers with no socks. He had nice legs. Not knobby like some men's, but strong calved and lean, with thighs that looked good in frayed cutoffs.

"Washing the car, huh?" He was looking at my bumper.

"I'm going to Asheville." But of course he knew that. "I don't like to go in a dirty car."

He squinted at the sky. "Well, it doesn't look like it's going to rain after all."

To say the tension between us was thick would have been an understatement. But it lasted less than another second because before I could take a breath to reply I heard the distant scrambling of claws on wood floor and a happy bark, and Cisco came bursting through the screen door and barreling down the steps. He was supposed to be in the back play yard with the other dogs, but he had apparently heard Buck's voice, come in through the dog door, and made a beeline for the front yard.

He skidded through the puddle, splashing

dirty water everywhere, did a sliding half turn, and flung himself on Buck, apparently trying to leap into his arms. I shouted, "Damn it, Cisco!" and Buck, recovering himself after one startled step backward, started laughing and ruffling Cisco's fur while Cisco added muddy paw prints to the front of Buck's shirt.

"This dog's going to think his name is 'Damn it,'" Buck observed, grinning, but I ignored him. I could hear the barking of the pack, which was following Cisco's trail through the house, and I rushed to slam the front door. By the time I returned, it was too late to scold Cisco, who was rolling on the ground while Buck rubbed his exposed underside. So I scolded Buck instead.

"Stop petting him! You're only encouraging him!"

"He just wanted to say hello." He turned his attention back to Cisco. "Didn't you, big fellow?"

"He tore a hole in my screen door!"

Buck chuckled and addressed Cisco. "Next time make sure the door's not locked, bud."

I scowled at him. "What are you doing here, anyway?"

He gave Cisco's chin a final scratch and stood, making a futile and halfhearted attempt to brush mud off his shorts. "I thought I should come by and apologize."

This surprised me and made me a little uncomfortable. "You don't owe me an apology."

"I meant to Cisco. For missing his show."

Cisco got up and shook the mud and grass out of his fur, and Buck ruffled his ears one more time. Buck glanced at me, eyes laughing. "Where's your hammer? I'll fix the door."

I brought cold sodas, because it was the civilized thing to do, and when Buck had finished tacking the screen back into its frame we sat on the porch steps and drank them. Cisco lay between us, which was always his position of choice, and panted his silly golden retriever grin.

"So how come you're not running Cisco in agility tomorrow?" Buck wanted to know.

"I'm tired of losing," I told him. "Anyway, the way he's been acting he'll be lucky if he gets to go at all. He's been nothing but trouble lately. You'd think he was raised by wolves."

"You know what they say about kids who act out," commented Buck. "Maybe he's unhappy at home."

I gave him a withering look. "Are you kidding me? This dog has a better life than half the human children in this county."

He couldn't disagree with me there. "I still think he has a lot of potential."

"I do too. But he's also got a lot to learn, especially in the manners department. That's why we're focusing on obedience this year."

As long as we were talking about dogs, everything was relaxed between us, easy and normal, so we kept up that topic as long as we could. I knew that was not why Buck had come over, though. I knew something bad was coming.

After a while, a silence fell. Buck looked down at the half-empty soda can he dangled between his knees, and he said, "We need to talk about something."

Everything about his demeanor had changed: his voice, his face, the set of his shoulders. Even Cisco noticed, and he stretched back his head and yawned. That's something dogs do when they are stressed.

I said, "I thought we were talking about something." But it was a feeble attempt at lightness, and I knew I couldn't carry it off.

"His name is John Michael Hendricks, age thirty-seven, four-fifty King Street, Gastonia, South Carolina. People call him Micky. Divorced, two kids. Pays child support now and then, arrested once for drunk driving, license suspended and restored after six months. Don't tell me I'm not doing my job, Raine."

I felt heat stain my cheeks. "Meg said he had a thing against Mexicans, was always shooting his mouth off about it. She practically kicked him out of the restaurant because of it the very night Manny was killed. He had a temper; you saw him."

"And maybe you also saw that he had a gun. If he had wanted to do harm to Rodriguez, he likely would've used it."

"Not if it was an accident. Not if it was a fight that got out of hand."

"Hendricks wasn't even driving his truck that night. He had an alibi for the time Rodriguez was killed."

"You don't know exactly when he was killed," I pointed out sharply. "You know as well as I do that you can't pinpoint a time of death to the minute, or even the hour. All you know is that he left work when everybody else did at three thirty and that his body was found at eight thirty. And Micky Hendricks only had an alibi from five o'clock on."

"The damage was on the wrong side of his

truck."

"Did you even look for damage on the other side?"

"Why would Micky Hendricks want to vandalize the construction site and put himself out of a job?"

He had me there. "I don't know. That's why they call it an investigation."

"That's also why Hendricks is not a suspect."

"He's not a suspect because you—or the FBI, or both of you—have already picked a suspect and you're going to make the facts fit your case whether it makes sense or not."

"You're stretching, Raine."

"And you don't call your theory a stretch?"

Buck's gaze was on the mountains. "Construction site vandalism is a pretty common modus operandi for ecoterrorists."

I let out an exasperated puff of breath. "Oh, for the love of—! You just won't let go, will you? Is that the way it's going to be around here from now on? Every time a purse gets snatched or a picnic basket is raided, blame it on the legendary wild man of the woods? You're just as bad as Rick, blaming that poor misplaced bear for every trampled rosebush and missing apple pie in this county." Beneath the ferocity of his knit brows I saw the faintest glimmer of mirth. "Not a good analogy, Raine. I saw what that bear did to the pickup truck, remember?"

Now it was my turn to frown. "You know what I mean."

In a moment he sighed. "Yeah, I do. Ever since you were a kid, if there was a cause to be championed or an underdog to be defended, there you were with both fists swinging." He looked at me. "Never made any difference whether you were right or wrong back then either."

"What makes you so all-fired certain I'm wrong?" I demanded, and the moment they were spoken I wanted to snatch the words back. The last thing in the world I really wanted was an answer to that question. Because I was afraid that there was one, and that it would be convincing, and that if it were I would have to face a truth I had been studiously avoiding since the moment I had heard Andy's name spoken two days ago.

Buck gazed again out over the still, shadowed lawn, the deep blue mountains. "Do you know what I do all day? Me and the fourteen other members of the Hanover County Sheriff's Department? We track down leads. Each and every piss ant little complaint, every rumor of a peeping Tom or a dog barking when it shouldn't have been or a suspicious character hanging around after a business closes or a car parked where it shouldn't be. We go out and we interview every witness and we write a full report and we take it back to the FBI and they run it through all their fact-correlating machinery and try to match it up against the profile they have of a known terrorist."

"Don't call him a terrorist."

"He blows things up, Raine," Buck replied evenly. "Andy Fontana is a terrorist."

My hand tightened on the soda can until my fingers caused a small, popping indentation in one side. I tried to relax my grip.

"In the past five days I've taken a report on a missing cell phone that somebody thinks they left on a picnic bench at one of the campgrounds. A .44-caliber pistol stolen out of a glove box. Camping supplies missing from somebody's shed."

I could hardly breathe. A cell phone left on a bench... Without looking at him, I whispered, "You could lose your job for telling me this."

"Yes, I could." But his tone didn't change. "Then add to that a construction site that's extensively vandalized, at least partially by human hands. The same evening a man is found dead in a ditch not two hundred yards from the site."

My heart thudded once, hard, against my rib cage. I was reminded that the accident had happened so close to where we had been. Manny might have been lying there, injured and dying, the whole time, and we never noticed.

"Now we've got evidence that it might not have been an accident. That the victim might have witnessed the vandalism. That he might have been killed because of it."

I was already shaking my head. "It wasn't Andy."

"Last night the Feed and Seed was broken into. Do you know what they sell at the Feed and Seed, Raine?"

"Dog food," I muttered, in barely a croak.

"Fertilizer. Twine. Kerosene. The makings of a bomb."

"Is that what was stolen?"

"Jeff stopped by after the Rotary meeting to pick up his sales slips—you know Rita does the books at home. He saw somebody in the store by the light of his headlights, and sure enough, the back door had been forced. Of course by the time we got there whoever it was had gone, and the place was such a mess Jeff is still trying to figure out what was taken, if anything."

Again my hand tightened on the soft drink can. "Then you don't know anything. None of this means anything!"

"The past couple of days we've added a new routine to our investigation. We've started personally interviewing storekeepers about unusual purchases, suspicious characters hanging around, that kind of thing. So last night I went into the Quick Mart and talked to Mil Sikes, who runs the place from six to midnight. At first he said that no, there hadn't been anything unusual unless you counted an increase in cigarette and beer sales from all the construction workers in town. Then he remembered this fellow who had come in off the Appalachian Trail—that's what he said, and couldn't describe him any better than long hair, army jacket, worn-out hiking boots and backpack. Bought a couple of packs of crackers and left. It was during the suppertime rush, eight or ten people in the store, most of them people he didn't know, paying for gas or picking up their evening smokes, so he didn't pay a lot of attention. But what was strange about it he said, was that a kid in line in front of him had picked up a sticker book— you know, the kind with all sorts of stickers in it like they decorate their book covers and backpacks with—and left it on the counter when he didn't have enough money to pay for it.

"After this guy left, the one from the Appalachian Trail, Will noticed the sticker book was gone. He thought it was kind of a strange thing for a grown man to shoplift, but since this guy had been the last customer of the rush, nobody in line after him, it had to be him. Then when Mil went out to empty the trash at the end of his shift he saw that sticker book in the Dumpster. He picked it up just long enough to see that the cellophane had been broken and a page torn out; then he tossed it back in. But I didn't have any trouble finding it. When I compared it to the other sticker books like it, it was easy to see there was only one page missing."

"The one with the rainbow sticker," I said softly.

My stomach was so tight I thought I might actually throw up. Cisco lifted his paw and put it on my knee, then let it slide off. I couldn't even meet my dog's eyes.

"Yeah, that's right. So far, the FBI hasn't been able to get any clear prints," he added.

Okay, I thought, trying to breathe. *Okay, so they have nothing. They have nothing.*

They had everything.

Buck threaded his fingers through Cisco's fur. He didn't look at me. "You remember back when crazy old Luke Stevens tried to block off Cutaway Sluice?"

I nodded. Cutaway Sluice was a section of the river where class-three rapids graduated to class five in less than five hundred yards. It was one of those "Whoa, what a ride!" sections of the river for rafters, and the calm water just above it was a popular put-in spot for kayakers and tubers from all over the state. "He claimed people were cutting across his property to get to it," I said. "Federal marshals finally had to come out and make him tear down the barricade."

"Yeah, but before that happened, his barn burned down, you remember?"

Again I nodded. "People always thought that might not have been an accident, but nobody tried very hard to find out. Everybody was so mad at Luke."

Buck said, "It wasn't an accident."

Of course I should have realized where he was going with this sooner. I said sharply, "You're not going to tell me Andy set that fire."

"That's exactly what I'm telling you."

"For God's sake, Buck, you can't just go around saying stuff that like! What would make you say something like that?"

"Because it's true."

"How do you know? How could you possibly know?"

Buck's attention was focused on the long, deep, golden parallel lines his stroking fingers were making in Cisco's fur. Cisco basked in the luxury, his eyes half closed in an ecstasy of contentment. Buck replied simply, "Because I helped him."

I couldn't speak. There was no way I could have made my voice work at that moment; I could barely remember to make my lungs move air in and out. I simply stared at him.

He lifted one shoulder in a slight shrug, not in dismissal, but more in discomfort. "Not that it makes any difference, but I didn't plan to burn down the barn. We figured—hell, you got to remember that it was us boys that were tubing down Cutaway Sluice every day of the week during the summer. As far as we knew, God had put the sluice there just for us, and we were more than a little pissed when this crazy old farmer thought he could block it off. So Andy and I decided to teach him a little lesson.

"All we planned was your everyday, run-of-the-mill vandalism. Just mess things up a little, leave a few well-thought-out words spray-painted on the side of the barn...at least that's what I thought the plan was. Maybe that's what Andy planned too at first, I don't know. So we got out there, we tossed stuff around, used up four or five spray-paint cans, messed with his tractor. About that time I was thinking what kind of trouble I would be in if my daddy ever found out, so I started trying to get Andy to haul ass out of there. But he found a ten-gallon can of gasoline and started pouring it over everything. I guess I tried to stop him, I don't know; I really just wanted to get clear away. I do know I didn't believe, not for a minute, that he would do what he did. I thought he was just, you know, making a mess.

"Then, next thing I knew he lit a match, and tossed it, and..." A breath, sharp and short, and it reminded me of the sound a fire might make, sucking all the oxygen out of the air. He had a fistful of Cisco's fur between his fingers, and his knuckles were white.

"That place went up like an atom bomb. All that dried timber, hay, turpentine, paint cans... It burned the hair off my arms before I could get back. I remember grabbing Andy by the shirt collar and screaming at him—'You fucking idiot, are you crazy?'—that kind of thing over and over while I was trying to drag him away. I mean, all I could think of was running, but he was like, I don't know, mesmerized. He just stood there, staring at it, like he couldn't take his eyes off it, and the way he looked—the expression on his face with the reflection from the flames making his skin look like it was on fire, and his eyes... Well, all you could see in his eyes was the fire. The way he looked was—I've never been able to describe it, but it was...I don't know, almost religious."

Buck stopped, and I thought that was it, that he wouldn't go on. I saw him unclench the fist that was wound around Cisco's fur and instead gently lift one of my dog's ears and massage it sweetly. Cisco groaned with pleasure.

Still Buck did not lift his eyes to me, or turn his head. He said, "You know what he said to me, while I was cussing at him and dragging at his arm and he wouldn't move? I mean, he was like a stone; he just stood there, watching the fire. He said, real calm like, 'Don't sweat it, man. These people have got to learn.' And then he kind of smiled, and he said, 'You know what the Bible says. And God gave Noah the rainbow sign; not the water but the fire next time.'"

I put my hand to my mouth, pressing hard, and I actually had to breathe through my fingers for several long, deep inhalations before I could speak. Finally I lowered my hand to Cisco's neck, and I stroked him lightly, my fingers only a few inches from Buck's. I knew Buck could see that my hand was unsteady, but I didn't care.

I said, "And you never told anybody about that night."

Now he looked at me. "Yeah," he said. "I told somebody. I told the FBI when they interviewed me about Andy fifteen years ago."

I closed my eyes slowly. When I opened them

again, I was surprised that my voice was almost—not quite, but almost—normal. "They asked me about that phrase," I said softly, "back then. The FBI agents, I mean. 'The fire next time.' I didn't know what it meant."

Buck was silent for a moment. "The rainbow didn't become a symbol for PCP until after Andy joined, did you know that? I think he might have been a lot higher up in the organization during college than you knew."

Rainbows on the bathroom mirror, on a foggy car windshield, on a grocery list with a heart. But I couldn't let my mind go there. I just couldn't.

"It's not from the Bible," I said. "It's from a song. A spiritual."

"I know. I looked it up."

"It's a popular song. A lot of people know it. It's about the flood, and how…" I trailed off, unable to finish.

"How God will cleanse the earth of wickedness one day?" Buck supplied. "Not with flood, but fire."

Cisco licked my hand. "Yeah."

And then Buck said, "Raine."

He said it in such a way that I had to meet his eyes. They were dark and troubled, and all I could think about was how many years I had been looking into those eyes, how well I knew every expression in them, how much the two of us had been through together.

He said, "I need to know. Do you still love him?"

I didn't answer. I could hardly believe I'd heard the question.

In an odd, kind of strained voice, he added,

"Because I never knew. I never knew whether it was me you loved, or him. All those years with you... I wanted to ask, but I was afraid of what the answer would be, I guess. You and Andy—you were always so tight, even as kids. You cared about the same things, you thought alike, and when you ended up together I wasn't surprised. I don't think anyone was. I guess the real surprise was when you married me. All this time, I couldn't help wondering...whether Andy was the one you really loved, and I was just the one you settled for."

I moved my hand away from Cisco's silky soft fur because it was far too close to Buck's hand. I answered in a voice that was stiff and cold and barely steady. "You have no right to ask me that. No man who cheats on his wife not once, but over and over again, has a right to ask that."

"I know I've screwed up," he said. "I know I've hurt you. But that's not what this is about."

What Buck didn't understand, what he would never understand, was that once you have been a woman betrayed, that's what everything is about.

I stood up. "I think you'd better go. I have a lot to do." Buck stood too, but on the step below me, so that our eyes were even. Cisco got up and stretched, curling his white-feathered tail over his back and rolling his tongue in a yawn.

Buck said, "After the chemical plant bombing, the FBI got a call. The caller said, 'And God gave Noah the rainbow sign; not the water but the fire next time.' I just learned that this morning."

I clasped my upper arms tightly and pressed my lips together. It didn't mean anything. Not a thing. Except that, fifteen years ago, it had been

Buck's statement that had broken the case for the FBI and put Andy on the Most Wanted list.

He said, "Anyway, that's why I had to ask...what I did. I'm sorry." He turned to leave.

"Buck."

He looked back at me. I said, "The FBI—they can trace cell phone calls, can't they?"

His expression gentled with regret. "Yeah, hon," he said. "They can." He took my face between his hands, and he kissed my forehead. "Good luck tomorrow," he said. "I'm sorry I can't be there."

The sweetness of that gesture made me want to cry.

Chapter Eleven

People get into competitive dog sports for all kinds of reasons. You'd think there would be just one reason: because you love dogs and want to have fun with them. But from what I can tell, that's hardly ever really it.

The first thing you'll notice at a dog show is that the overwhelming majority of handlers are women. A lot of people have speculated about why that is. Believe or not, one of the most popular theories is that women have more spare time for hobbies. Ask any mother of three who works a full-time job and takes care of the house, the kids, the pets and a husband how much spare time she has to train dogs.

Another theory is that women have more patience, and that their predisposition for nurturing and problem solving makes them more successful at dog training than the average man. Maybe. Raising kids and training dogs probably have a lot more in common than most people realize.

Maybe it has to do with that old saw about "finding your tribe." In the world of dogs, everyone has one thing in common, and that's all you need. Maybe it has to do with finding a little bit of control in a world in which everything else is out of your control. Maybe it's because, at a dog show, there aren't any fax machines or switchboards and the only computers belong to the scorekeepers. There isn't any laundry to be done or dishes to be washed, and there are hardly ever any husbands.

At a dog show you eat cheeseburgers and funnel cakes and don't give a second thought to what they are doing to your figure—or your digestion, for that matter. You spend ten dollars on a knotted fleece tug toy that your dog might play with once, and congratulate yourself on having gotten a bargain. You sit in the sun and watch some of the most beautiful creatures God ever made show off what they're best at, and you are surrounded by people who are as fascinated by the whole thing as you are.

For me it's probably all of this and a little bit more. For me a dog show is like one of those Zen meditations where the entire universe can be revealed in a breath. It's an island of safety where real life can't follow. Here a ticket to heaven can be bought with a thirty-second run, here all the world is governed by AKC rules and here the only thing that matters is the adoration in your dog's eyes when he looks up at you.

Even if the FBI had closed down the road to Asheville, I would not have allowed that to keep me away from this show.

After four restless hours of sleep, I decided to leave for Asheville a little earlier than planned. I was there before the gates opened to the agricultural center where the show was being held. By six a.m. I had set up my portable shade canopy in a prime viewing spot beside the agility ring, arranged the two mesh dog crates—with their cool mats, fans, ice water and chew toys—inside, set up my canvas chair, cooler and thermos of coffee and slathered myself with sunscreen. I walked both Cisco and Mischief in the dewy dawn, helped the ring crew set up the agility course and was the first person in line for a ham, cheese and egg biscuit when the vending cart opened. I took Mischief over the practice jump and Cisco through the entire set of novice obedience exercises, twice. They were ready. I was ready. We were pumped.

I swear, if I could have lived there, in this netherworld of dogs and fried food and blue-ribbon rosettes, I would have gladly walked out on everything I knew from my old life and never looked back.

At least, that's how I felt that day.

Maude arrived a little before seven and was amazed by both my presence—I am notorious for cutting my arrival at shows close—and my energy. I helped her set up in the space I had reserved next to me, and we walked down to the pavilion to get a copy of the conformation show schedule. Already the merchant vendors had most of their tents up, and my adrenaline started to soar. This was going to be a great day; I could just feel it.

According to the schedule, the golden retrievers would be showing at ten, and the group competitions wouldn't begin until after lunch, which worked out perfectly. Although neither

Maude nor I would be showing in conformation, we liked to watch the competition and to keep up with who's who in the world of our favorite breeds.

A major all-breed dog show is very much like a three-ring circus. While agility is going on in one ring, obedience is taking place in another, and breed judging is going on in the pavilion. Because I was showing Cisco in obedience, I would miss being able to watch the first round of agility, and because I was showing Mischief in agility, I wouldn't be able to watch Maude show River in advanced obedience. Those were the choices you made.

Judging for novice obedience got started at eight. And that's when everything began to go downhill.

I quickly saw that I had made a mistake by setting up so close to the agility ring. The advanced levels of agility were already under way when I unzipped the door of Cisco's portable crate and took him out to begin warm ups. Of course he noticed all the dogs running, jumping and barking. Of course he wanted to join them. Even though the obedience ring was far down the hill and hidden from the agility venue, Cisco kept looking over his shoulder longingly, and then at me as though wondering whether I had lost my sense of direction.

Maude stood well outside the obedience ring to watch, and she gave me a subtle thumbs-up as our number was called and we entered the ring for judging. I wasn't worried. This was going to be piece of cake.

The novice obedience exercises are really very

simple. The judge calls out a series of commands, like "Heel forward, right turn, left turn, halt," and judges you on how precisely your dog executes each command. You perform the exercises first on leash, and then off leash. After all the dogs have been judged on the moving exercises, everyone is called back into the ring for the long sit and the long down. A perfect score is 200, and points are taken off for every mistake. Like I said, piece of cake.

Cisco has a beautiful, prancing stride and I figured that might distract the judge from the fact that he didn't exactly keep his shoulder perfectly aligned with my knee the whole time. He swung his butt out on the sit, which cost us a point. But otherwise, I was pleased with our performance.

Then it was time to take off the leash.

The reason so many novice handlers fail this exercise is that they try to show too soon. Their dogs simply aren't ready for off-leash work. But Cisco had been working off leash since he was a puppy. He had been running agility for over a year. He did wilderness search and rescue. There was no reason in the world he couldn't walk around an obedience ring for three minutes off leash.

I unsnapped the lead and Cisco remained sitting at my side. His ears were up and he was grinning happily, and I'm sure he knew I was pleased with him. The judge said, "Forward."

I said, "Cisco, heel," and took off with a brisk striding step with Cisco right beside me.

The judge said, "About-turn," and I executed a crisp pivot on my heel, turning in the other direction.

Cisco kept going.

I saw it all out of the corner of my eye. His ears went forward, his tail swung upward and he broke into a gallop. I swung around just in time to see him leap over the ring gating and start racing around the outside of the ring like a thoroughbred at the Kentucky Derby.

Someone shouted "Loose dog!" but too late. Dogs and people scattered everywhere as Cisco blurred around the ring, a streak of gold and white with ears and tail flying, once, twice, and then I screamed, "Cisco, here!"

There must have been something in my voice that brooked no argument, because Cisco tore up tufts of grass with the abruptness of his about-turn. Tongue lolling happily, he raced back to me, sailed over the ring gating and back into the ring, circled me once in a cloud of dust, and then came to stop with a perfect sit directly in front of me. He gazed up at me, panting and grinning, looking as proud as if he had just won the world cup.

I just stood there with my mouth open on a half-indrawn breath, paralyzed with shock. The judge looked at me with eyebrows raised high.

"Nice recall," she said. "I hope you'll try again when you have more control over your dog off leash. You're excused."

I managed to mutter, "Thank you, judge," as I snapped on Cisco's lead and marched him out of the ring. My cheeks were burning, and even though the laughter I heard as I passed was good-natured, it was still laughter. A few people said, "Great dog," but I barely managed a civil response. The last thing I would have called Cisco right then was "great."

As Maude fell into step beside me, I said through clenched teeth, "Not a word."

"Oh, I wouldn't," she assured me. "I wouldn't say a word."

I was walking so fast that even Cisco had to trot to keep up with me, but Maude's stride was effortless.

"But if I did say a word," she added, "two words, actually, they would be 'lovely recall.' "

I gave her a quelling glare and proceeded up the hill in silence.

By the time I shoved Cisco into his crate and zipped it closed, I think he was starting to figure out that I had not found his performance amusing. I left him to think things over alone and took Mischief with me as I went off to find the funnel cake vendor.

There is very little in this world that fried dough drenched in powdered sugar can't cure, and by the time I returned to my campsite I was feeling a little more sanguine. For one thing, not having to show Cisco in the group obedience exercises meant I would be able to watch more of the breed judging in the conformation pavilion. For another, as I approached my tent with Mischief in a perfect trot beside me, I saw that Sonny and Mystery were already there, waiting for me. I waved, and Sonny waved back.

"How did you know where to find me?" I asked as I approached.

"I didn't," she replied, nodding toward Cisco's crate. "Mystery found Cisco. What is he pouting about?"

She was always saying things like that, attributing human emotions to dogs, but what would make her think he was pouting I couldn't guess. I explained about the fiasco in the obedience ring as I put Mischief back in her crate with a chew bone. I even managed to make it sound as funny as it probably seemed to everyone else.

Still, I appreciated the fact that Sonny didn't laugh. Instead, she nodded thoughtfully. "Well," she said, "I'm sure you understand that he wasn't really certain what you wanted him to do when you took the leash off. After all, he says that the last time he was at a show you wanted him to run fast and jump over things."

Now, that actually made sense, and I gave Sonny an appreciative look. I had been training Cisco for a year in agility, and at every show we went to, the minute I took the leash off, that was his signal to get ready to run. I had spent only a couple of months training him in obedience, and I had done even that perfunctorily. Maude had been right; the change was too abrupt, and Cisco wasn't ready.

"Also," added Sonny, still looking at Cisco, who could be seen through the mesh of the crate lying with his head on his paws and looking very much like he was pouting, "he finds the whole thing incredibly boring. He says he has more important things to do."

I couldn't prevent a downward turn of my Lips. "Oh, yeah? Like what?"

She hesitated, then said, "Like chasing coyotes."

A chill went through me, and I stared at her. "What did you say?"

She looked studious for a minute, her head

cocked toward Cisco's crate as though she was actually listening to him. Then she looked at me and shrugged. "That's the best I can do. Coyotes. I don't think it's quite right, though. Are there really coyotes around here?"

I was looking over her shoulder, and my heart began to thud, hard, painfully. I said, "Yes. And here come two of them now."

Chapter Twelve

I couldn't believe it. In my worst pepperoni-pizza-with-anchovies-and-pineapple-induced nightmares I could not have come up with anything like this. Coming toward me across the parking lot was Special Agent Tom Dickerson accompanied by a man I did not know. Both were dressed for the occasion in the finest of dog show casual wear. The stranger wore a suit and dark sunglasses that practically screamed "government agent," and Mr. Dickerson, who had opted for less subtlety, wore pressed khakis and a dark Windbreaker with the letters FBI stenciled across the upper-left chest and the back.

It was like one of those dreams where you try to run and your legs are like taffy; you try to scream and your vocal cords are paralyzed. I watched these leviathans from the Real World invade my Island of Safety with a sinking, helpless sense of sanity spinning out of control. I watched all eyes following them as they bore down on me—the eyes of people I knew, people who knew and trusted me—and I was rooted to the spot, unable to run, unable to hide.

Unsmiling, Dickerson said, "Miss Stockton, this is Simon Meeks from the Department of Homeland Security."

Homeland Security. My face actually felt cold as the blood drained out of it.

Mr. Simon Meeks held out his credentials, which I didn't even look at. I could feel Sonny staring at me, and Mystery, sensing her alarm, pressed close to her mistress and stiffened, tail curled and ears forward. Afraid she was about to attack one of the men, I said hoarsely to Sonny, "Watch your dog."

Sonny's hand tightened on the slack leash and she took a step back with Mystery. Cisco stood up in his crate, watchful, his tail held low and swishing slowly, uncertainly, back and forth.

Meeks put his ID away when he saw I wasn't interested, and said, "Please come with us, Miss Stockton."

My senses kicked in with an automatic instinct to protect my dogs, if not myself. Outraged, I replied, "Don't be ridiculous! I'm in the middle of a show! I'm not leaving my dogs!"

About then, the impact of Mr. Meeks' words, and the cold, humorless tone in which they were said, hit me in the chest, and I couldn't say anything else. Cisco whined. I felt like Alice in Wonderland; everything was growing very small.

I think one of the men must have moved toward me, because Sonny stepped forward abruptly. "I'm Miss Stockton's lawyer. May I see a warrant?"

I wanted to cry, I was so grateful. But I was also very worried about Mystery's protective body posture. I said, "Sonny, it's okay…"

And Meeks said, "We hadn't planned on needing one. However…"

"Did you bring a crate for Mystery?" I asked.

Sonny amazed me with a brisk, authoritative, "Mystery, lie down." Mystery dropped to the ground before the words were completely spoken, her head on her paws, her ears relaxed, her eyes watchful.

Dickerson said, "At this point you're not under arrest, Miss Stockton, but you're certainly welcome to have your attorney with you. We would like to ask you a few more questions about People for a Clean Planet."

Sonny could not hide her astonishment. "What in the world would Raine know about that?"

I said, a little hoarsely, "Ask me here. I can't leave my dogs."

Dickerson said, "Do you mean you haven't mentioned your involvement with Andy Fontana to your lawyer?" Sonny looked at me as though she had never seen me before, and I couldn't blame her. "Andy Fontana—the bomber?"

I said, "She's not my lawyer."

Sonny continued to stare at me.

Meeks said, "Please come with us now, Miss Stockton."

I couldn't deal with the shock and disbelief in Sonny's eyes. I didn't have time for an explanation. I said, "Watch my dogs. If I'm not back by the time Maude finishes showing River, tell her— Tell her to take Cisco and Mischief home for me. But I'll be back. It won't take long. It'll be okay."

I fell into place between the two men and had

taken only a few steps when Sonny said, "Wait."

She still looked stunned and horrified, and her gaze wouldn't meet mine. But apparently the lawyer in her was still at work because she demanded of Special Agent Dickerson, "Where are you taking her?"

He pulled out a card and handed it to her. "We'll be interviewing Miss Stockton at the Asheville office of the FBI. You're welcome to join us there. Just give your name to the front desk and you'll be cleared through."

I said tightly, "Stay with my dogs."

Sonny took the card.

I repeated, "Sonny, don't get involved in this."

She still couldn't meet my eyes, and I turned away quickly before she could say anything. "Let's go, then," I said to Dickerson.

And so I was escorted off the grounds with an FBI agent on one side and an investigator from the Department of Homeland Security on the other. I didn't look left, I didn't look right, I didn't look back. But I could feel the eyes of everyone in the whole world following me. And I wanted to die.

I knew there was a difference between an informal interview, like the one Special Agent Dickerson had conducted at my home earlier in the week, and a real one. I had some vague understanding of the fact that material witnesses—a category in which for some reason the FBI seemed to have decided I should be included—had to be officially logged. That was the purported reason for taking me "downtown," as it were.

That was not, however, the real reason. Special Agent Dickerson had not brought along a rep from the Department of Homeland Security just to be neighborly. The real reason was to humiliate me in front of my friends, intimidate me with a display of official power, and scare me half to death. This I knew beyond a doubt, and it was working, on all three counts.

I kept thinking I might never see my dogs again.

It wasn't that the men treated me badly. They took me into a nice air-conditioned interview room with beige carpeting and cushions on the chairs. They brought me coffee, which I didn't drink. They brought in a pleasant female agent who was supposed to make me feel comfortable. They asked whether I wanted to wait for my lawyer. I said I didn't, and I tried to remind myself that the only reason they mentioned a lawyer was to worry me. After all, the only people who needed lawyers were people who were in trouble.

I was a judge's daughter. I knew these things.

They started asking me all the questions they had asked me fifteen years ago, about my relationship with Andy. I don't remember what I said. None of those questions had anything to do with what they really wanted from me.

Then Special Agent Dickerson, who had apparently decided to take on the role of Good Cop for this portion of the performance, said, "I'm sure you're aware of the series of fires and explosions that took place between the time you graduated from college and the time of the chemical plant bombing that killed four people, all of them accredited to Andy Fontana."

I said, "But none of them ever proven."

He nodded. "Didn't you ever wonder why we

linked all of them to him?"

I said nothing. Perhaps the smartest thing I'd done all day.

"The offending party—whether it was the headquarters of a trucking company that transported toxic waste, the paper plant that was cutting down too many trees, the developer that was destroying a wetland—always received the mark of the rainbow, sometimes on a postcard in the mail, sometimes painted on a building, sometimes e-mailed. After the chemical plant bombing, the FBI here in Asheville actually received a phone call. The caller quoted from a song. 'Not the water but the fire next time.' I believe the last agents who talked to you mentioned that."

Again I stayed quiet.

Dickerson went on, "Of course a lot of this is common knowledge. It all came out during the investigation fifteen years ago. But what you might not know is that even before that, back when Fontana was living in Hanover County with his grandparents, there were a series of fires locally over the years...some of them small enough, or ordinary enough, to slip under the law enforcement radar. But they all had one thing in common."

He wanted me to say it, but I wouldn't. So Meeks supplied, "A rainbow was found painted or drawn somewhere nearby in about seventy percent of the cases we investigated."

Special Agent Dickerson said, "Have you noticed that particular sign, the rainbow, anywhere it shouldn't have been in the last week or so?"

I answered, "Yes." You don't lie to the FBI...or the Department of freakin' Homeland Security.

The two agents glanced at each other. Dickerson asked, "Where?"

I told him, "On the bumper of my car," and because it was late and I was tired and they knew all this anyway, I went on, "It was a sticker. I washed it off. I only have dog-related bumper stickers on my car."

"Any idea how it got there?"

"No."

"Would it surprise you to know that we found Andy Fontana's fingerprints on a cellophane wrapper of a book of stickers that once contained a rainbow sticker?"

I said, "Yes," which seemed to surprise them, because the female agent looked up from her note taking and wanted to know why.

I answered, "Because Andy's not that stupid. If he were, he wouldn't have managed to elude capture all these years."

Dickerson considered that. "There's a difference between stupidity and recklessness. Maybe he believes he can't be caught."

"Maybe you didn't find any fingerprints."

Special Agent Dickerson smiled. "Actually, we did. And they were Fontana's."

Then Meeks spoke up. "Would you like to know where else we found Fontana's fingerprints, Miss Stockton?" My chest hurt. I couldn't breathe, much less speak. Meeks answered in an absolutely expressionless voice, "In your kitchen. In your bedroom, in your living room, hallway, bathroom, on your back door, even on one of the cages where you keep your dogs—in fact, all over your house."

Oh, my God, oh, my God... That was what I wanted to say. What I couldn't say. And I knew, the judge's daughter in me knew, I should not only ask for a lawyer, I should scream for one. But in fact the only words that came out of my mouth, on a big gust of choked-back breath, were, "How did you get in my house? You can't just come into my house!"

Meeks smiled. Or it was something that resembled a smile. "We had a warrant. Thanks to your husband, we had enough evidence to dust for fingerprints. We did not, however," he continued, "have enough evidence to search your house for anything else. Yet." No mistaking the emphasis he put on that word, or the cold certainty in his eyes when he said it. "I would also like to say that the Hanover County Sheriff's Department was on the scene the entire time, making sure we didn't overstep the boundaries of the warrant, just in case you're worried." Again he smiled. "Lucky lady. You seem to be popular over there."

Buck. Buck had done this. He had let them into my house.

Something cold and dispassionate started to creep through me. I started to understand where this could go. I started to realize that I really might never see my dogs again.

And that simply was not going to happen.

I dug my fingers into my crossed arms, and eventually the trembling stopped. For a long time I simply listened to the sound of my own breathing. Then I asked, quietly, steadily, "What do you want from me?"

With as much of a show of kindness as he was

apparently capable, Special Agent Dickerson said, "Miss Stockton, I'm going to be up-front with you. You are not a suspect in this case. I honestly don't believe you are anything more than another one of Fontana's victims. The fingerprints on the outside of your back door might even suggest that Fontana let himself into your house, perhaps without your knowledge, and that's how his fingerprints came to be found all over your belongings."

"On the other hand," said Meeks, "there was no sign of forced entry. And our records don't show that you ever reported a crime. So perhaps what we're looking at here is less of a break-in than a...rendezvous?"

"Of course," added Dickerson with just the right note of regret, "there's also the evidence you withheld from a homicide investigation. You haven't exactly cooperated with our investigation here, Miss Stockton. To some people it might even appear you've interfered with it. When you add everything together, and view it all in the light of your past relationship with a known criminal, it's difficult to know what to make of you."

"You know something?" I said. "I've been around law enforcement all my life. You don't have to play these games with me. Just tell me what you want."

Dickerson regarded me steadily. "Okay, fair enough. But first I want you to understand something. We wanted Andy Fontana because he was high up in a subversive organization and directly responsible for a number of bombings and at least four deaths that we know of. But that's not what kept him on the top ten most-wanted list for fifteen years. And we didn't devote the kind of resources that we did to break up PCP just to roust a few tree huggers. Surely you had to suspect that, Miss Stockton, even back then. Like you said, you come from a law enforcement background."

I carefully unscrewed the cap on the bottle of water that someone had placed on the table beside me at the beginning of the interview, and I drank. I replaced the cap and waited for him to go on. He did.

"There's an old saying: Follow the money. In the case of PCP, we followed it far enough to find some really bad guys. What you heard on the news was that the PCP financing came from bank robberies and drug deals. Some of it did. But a lot of it came from favors."

He waited for me to ask. I tried to stop myself from complying. But I had to say, "What kind of favors?"

That seemed to be the opening Meeks had been waiting for. "The question is not so much what kind of favors, but for whom. And the answer to that is arms dealers, military training camps..." He held my gaze. "PCP recruited some very talented people, and your boyfriend was just one of them. The organization might have looked homegrown, but it was controlled by, and served, a much larger purpose. None of this is in dispute, Miss Stockton," he added, as I began to shake my head furiously. "We have independent confessions from a variety of sources."

"What's important for you to know," Dickerson said, "is that when the net started to close around Fontana, he had an escape route. Didn't you ever wonder how your hometown boy, who—according to your testimony fifteen years ago—had never even had a passport, managed to evade the FBI, the CIA, and the governments of at least six cooperating nations to disappear without a trace?"

I swallowed. I had wondered that. A lot.

Meeks said, "He had friends in very high places. The kind of friends who take care of their own because they know that a talent like his can always be put to use, anywhere in the world. And because Fontana had an ace in the hole."

I waited. The three interrogators, including the woman, studiously avoided looking at me. Finally, they seemed to come to some unspoken conclusion, and Meeks said flatly, "When Andy Fontana disappeared, so did the bankroll of the PCP. Now Fontana has come back for the money. And we believe you know where it is."

The sound that came out of my mouth was somewhere between a shriek of laughter and a gasp of outrage. "Are you kidding me? Are you freakin' kidding me? You followed me down here, you pulled me out of a show and dragged me into your office, you kept me here asking me the same stupid questions over and over again for half a day and it's all because you think I know where Andy Fontana buried a hundred and thirty-two million dollars?"

Someone said, "Please sit down, Miss Stockton."

I had not even realized I was standing. I did not sit down. "Look at me!" I gestured to my dusty T-shirt, my faded, baggy jeans, my running shoes. "Do I look like someone who knows how to put her hands on that kind of money? If I knew where a hundred and thirty-two million dollars was buried—even if I believed it ever existed!—would I be training dogs and stalking bears for a living? Are you people insane?"

And then I sank back into my chair, breathing hard, looking from one to the other of them in absolute disbelief.

Agent Meeks said, "No one ever said the money was in cash, Miss Stockton, or that he buried it."

"We do, however, know for a very close certainty that it is hidden somewhere in the mountains around Hanover County. And the only person who knows those mountains better than Andy Fontana is you."

The hilarity that had been such a welcome release was slowly replaced by dread and a familiar puzzlement. "If it's not cash—what?"

Again a shared glance. The female agent, whose name I was to leave the room without ever remembering, answered, "Diamonds."

I was picturing a treasure chest filled with glittering jewels, and my astonishment must have shown in my eyes because Meeks explained, "Diamonds are the currency of choice for a lot of illegal underground organizations. They're small, durable, easy to conceal, virtually untraceable, and they never depreciate in value. In this particular case, the entire treasury of the PCP could have been concealed in a soda can."

"Imagine trying to find a single soda can in the Nantahala Forest," put in Dickerson.

I swallowed hard. "Andy...didn't know anything about diamonds."

"He wouldn't have to. The transaction was

made by another member of the organization. All Andy had to do was keep the diamonds safe."

"Okay." I drew in a breath through my teeth, crossing my arms, trying to think. "Okay, so even if Andy did have these diamonds, and even if he did get this far with them...what makes you think he didn't take them with him when he left the country all those years ago? What makes you think they're still there?"

It was Meeks who finally spoke. "Fontana might have been out of the public eye for the past fifteen years, and out of our reach for most of them, but his name has popped up now and then in connection with one terrorist group or another." His gaze held mine, hard. "Most of them Middle East based. He's got talent, he's got opportunity, he's got access. But what these groups need most is funding. And now he has that."

"Our intelligence is that Fontana has promised to deliver a gold mine to a certain Middle Eastern organization before the end of the month," added Dickerson. "It's his buy-in straight to the top."

Said Meeks, quietly, "You could finance a nuclear strike with that kind of money."

I said stiffly, "You're wrong. You're all wrong. All Andy ever wanted to do was stop the destruction of our natural resources. He's not a..." Buck's voice: He blows things up, Raine. He's a terrorist.

"He's not what you say," I finished. But by then the words sounded hollow. "And there aren't any diamonds."

"Then why did he come back here?" asked Dickerson reasonably. "If not for the diamonds—what?"

Into my miserable silence, the woman spoke up. "Obviously, we don't think you know the exact location of the diamonds, Raine." She was the only one who called me by my first name. "At least not consciously. If we did, you'd be facing a long prison sentence for accessory to a federal crime. What we do realize, and what we've known from the beginning, is that if we send an army of federal agents into the woods to search, Andy Fontana can elude us for months—for years. We can't close down a national forest. All he has to do is outwait us, and we think he's prepared to do just that."

"But you can go in," said Dickerson. "You know places in those woods we could spend the rest of our lives looking for."

"You know the same places Fontana does. You can lead us to them," said the woman.

Meeks added, "It's imperative that those diamonds not leave this country."

Slowly understanding, I said, "That's why you let him get this far. This was your plan all along."

Silence was my confirmation.

I said after a time, "He won't let me, or anyone else, get near him."

"Actually," said Dickerson, "we think he will. We think he wants to see you. After all, he's tried to contact you on more than one occasion."

I said nothing. I felt a sourness rising in my throat that was half anger, half fear.

"Fontana won't leave these mountains without the diamonds," Meeks said, "and we can't let him leave with them. What are you going to do, Miss Stockton?"

I drew in a deep breath and let it out slowly.

"I'm tired," I said. "I have dogs to take care of. I can't believe you've kept me here all day for this. You've wasted my time and yours. The Nantahala Forest is not like a department store, where you can go shopping for what you need—squirrels and foxes here, trout fishing there, good hiding place for diamonds over there. It's over a thousand square miles of wilderness with a topography that changes every year, and there is no way I could possibly figure out where Andy Fontana may or may not have hidden something fifteen years ago. You don't need a tracker; you need a psychic."

I stood. "Can I go now?"

A hesitation, another shielded exchanged look, and then the two men stood as well. Dickerson said, "Of course. You were never under detention."

Meeks handed me his card. "Maybe you'll think about it, and if anything occurs to you—anything at all that might be of help—you'll give us a call."

I took the card reluctantly and stuffed it into my pocket without looking at it. I started toward the door and then looked back. "Let me ask you something. What did my husband tell you about me?"

It was the woman who answered. "He said you were very loyal to people you love."

I left the room.

Maude was waiting for me in the lobby of the building. She put her arm around my shoulders and we walked in silence into the late afternoon heat. She said, "Sonny took the dogs home. She has that big van."

I nodded, but I couldn't look at her. I felt so

bruised and beaten I could hardly find my voice. "How did you and River do?"

She squeezed my shoulders. "First place."

I turned and hugged her hard and tried not to cry.

A cacophony of happy barking greeted me when I finally made it home. I went first to Cisco and Mischief, who were safely secured in a kennel run as Maude had instructed Sonny. I sat down on the concrete floor and let them crawl all over me, wiggling and licking me and panting happily, while I hugged them close and rubbed my face into the sweet, clean, sunshine-pure smell of their coats. It had been a lifetime since Cisco jumped the ring gating, a century since Mischief had escaped her crate and raided the kitchen. At that moment I didn't think I could ever be angry with them about anything again.

Mary Ruth had already fed, watered and exercised all the dogs, but I still went from door to door, passing out dog biscuits and saying good night in a familiar ritual that might have meant more to me this night than any other. I took Cisco and Mischief to the house and spent a long silent time just walking through it, running my fingertips over the film of white powder that dusted every surface, noticing and trying not to notice how everything seemed just a little misplaced, touched, rearranged.

I released Magic and Majesty from their crates and reveled in another orgy of enthusiastic greeting. I tried not to imagine their distress when their house was invaded by strangers and they were locked away, helpless to protect themselves. I apologized over and over to them, burying my face in their fur and trying not to cry. But the good thing about being a dog, I suppose, is an extremely poor long-term memory. They had already forgotten whatever traumas they might have endured, and all they wanted was a romp in the backyard.

I let the dogs out and while they were gone took a bucket of soapy water and a sponge and wiped down every surface of my house. Then I went upstairs and stood under the shower until the hot water ran out. But I still didn't feel entirely clean.

There were two messages on my answering machine, and neither one of them was from Buck.

Rick's voice came first. "Hey, Raine. You won't believe this one. Dexter Franklin reported a bear tried to rip the front fender off his truck this morning. Said he got a good look at it, even took a shot at it, but didn't hit it. I know you don't want to hear this, but this is a bona fide eyewitness sighting with damage, and that makes four we can verify. You know what's got to be done. I just wanted to give you a heads-up. Talk to you later."

I frowned, replayed the message and frowned again. Dexter Franklin? He was way on the other side of the county from Valley Street, and why in the world would a bear try to rip a fender off a truck, anyway? For some reason, I got a flash of Dexter stalking out of the Feed and Seed muttering to himself, and then later parked on the side of the road by the construction site, arguing with somebody.

When was that, anyway? Wednesday?

Dexter peeling out of the Feed and Seed in his white pickup truck. A bear trying to rip the front fender off his truck. It was crazy. It didn't make sense.

And since when didn't a general contractor carry a crowbar in his tool box?

My head really hurt now.

The second message was from Sonny, sounding tired and strained. "Raine, please call me when you get this. I'm so sorry about what happened this morning. The last thing I wanted to do was leave you stranded. I want you to know I tried to get a lawyer for you, but he called back and said you had refused counsel. His name is Richard Marshall in case you change your mind. I got a little bit of information about what's going on from Maude but—Raine, I hope you understand, we can't have you on the board of Save the Mountains any longer. I—"

I deleted the message.

Sometimes, when a trial goes on longer than expected, or when jurors are sequestered without warning or are inconvenienced in other ways, they blame the defendant. Their sympathies, which might have formerly been with the defense, almost always switch to the prosecution, almost as if they are thinking, "Well, if that guy hadn't screwed up we wouldn't be here in the first place, so let's just get this over with." Jury strategists recognize this phenomenon and sometimes try to use it to their advantage.

I understood that Dickerson and Meeks had employed a version of the same strategy with me today. They had embarrassed me in front of my peer group and deprived me of a day with my dogs—which, for me, was more of a hardship than jail—and now even my friends were afraid of being associated with me. And it was all because of Andy. I should have been furious, fed up and at the end of my patience.

I was all of those things, but not with Andy.

I dialed Buck's cell phone. He was on duty, and his caller ID apparently told him it was me. He said, in answering, "Hey."

My voice was shaking. "He was your best friend, Buck. He was your best friend and you turned him in all those years ago. The authorities never would have made the connection between Andy and that song if you hadn't told them about the barn. You kept quiet when it suited you, and then you turned him in."

Buck said nothing.

I tried to breathe. I tried to remain calm. A lost cause. "You told them about my car," I said finally. "You told the FBI about the sticker."

Silence, even longer this time.

"Damn it, Buck, they came into my house! My dogs were here, all by themselves, and you let strangers come in here, toss through my things, take fingerprints..." A catch in my voice embarrassed me and terrified me because I thought I was going to cry. I would not cry. Not in front of him. So I stopped speaking.

Finally Buck said, quietly, heavily, "What did you expect from me, Raine? I'm a cop."

I had breath for one more sentence. I said, "You son of a bitch."

And I hung up the phone.

Before I went to bed I opened my mother's jewelry box and pushed aside the few pieces of costume jewelry I owned. Buck had made me put my mother's good pieces in a safe-deposit box long ago. Finally I found the charm bracelet that once held the key to Andy's heart.

That key, of course, was no longer there. I hadn't expected it to be.

Nonetheless, I spent a long time fingering the charms, remembering them, thinking about them. I took the bracelet to bed with me, and I fell asleep holding it. When I woke up, Cisco was standing over me, barking in my face, and the woods were on fire.

Chapter Thirteen

B y the time I reached the ranger station it was almost dawn, although you couldn't tell it because black smoke obscured the sky. My headlights were swallowed up by it, and the distant flash of red and blue lights was lost in it. I could hear helicopters beating close by, a reassuring sound.

I pulled into a parking lot filled with cars and forest service jeeps; the blaze of the building and parking lot lights illuminated the silhouettes of people rushing back and forth. I got out of the car and set the alarm. Cisco was in the back, along with his search and rescue vest, his tracking harness and my pack. Before I left the house I'd stuffed some extra power bars—both canine and human—into the pack, and a supply of chlorine water-purifying tablets. I didn't know how long I'd be gone.

Though the smoke wasn't so bad here, the night still smelled like a stale cigar, with undertones of crisp pine and cured hardwood, burning slowly. The odor made my eyes water.

The tiny office was a madhouse. I spoke to the

people I knew and nodded to the ones I didn't as I edged toward the front where Rick, with two other rangers I didn't know, was bent over a map. He glanced up and saw me.

"Raine, good, I'm glad you're here. Jake, Pete, you know Raine Stockton? She's got the search dog."

We exchanged greetings and, my chest tightening with urgency, I said, "Do you need us to go in?"

Rick shook his head. "Just stand by for now. I think we're going to be okay, but you never know when some damn fool is going to take off right into the path of a forest fire. We've got more search and rescue teams on the way."

"What about the campgrounds?"

"We're evacuating them now. Word is that they're not in any danger, but we can't take chances." He spoke to the two men. "So you guys help secure sectors three and four, and maintain radio contact." He gave me a weary, worried smile as the two rangers gathered up their equipment and left. "I guess this is what disaster drills are for."

"I could see the fire from my house. It looked like the whole back side of the mountain was going up."

"You'll be okay. The fire would have to jump three creeks and change direction to get to you."

I knew that. Nonetheless I had called Maude and Mary Ruth to begin moving the dogs to the vet's on the other side of town. Like Rick had said, we couldn't take any chances.

"What happened, Rick?"

He passed a hand over his eyes, which were as

red and bloodshot as mine no doubt were. "It looks like it started when the construction crew working on that utility road started burning brush last night."

"Burning brush? We're not issuing burn permits."

"Yeah, I know, and we could shut them down for that, but the foreman insists it wasn't his men. I'm about half persuaded to believe him since what were they doing burning at ten o'clock at night anyway? So while the fire department was busy with that one, another fire broke out here"— he stabbed a point on the map with his finger— "twice as big as the first one. It's been like that all night, a new fire every hour." He looked grim. "It's starting to look like they're being set deliberately, probably by kids. If so, they're facing some serious jail time. We're managing to keep the fires under control, and I don't think we're looking at any major property damage, but the cost in terms of resources and tourism..." He shook his head. "I don't know how many hundreds of acres we're going to lose."

I studied the map. "Are those red marks where the fires are?"

"Where they started. They're spreading west-northwest."

"In a circle," I murmured, "around the middle of the mountain."

"More or less. There are a few gaps here and there." He pointed. "The worst part is the smoke. This time of year everything is so thick and green that it's a slow burn. The firefighters can't work without respirators and they have to take a lot of breaks. This one could take days, Raine."

"Are you sure you don't need me right now?"

"I could use you to mind the phone, but Harriet is on her way. If you need to go back and watch your place, I understand. Just keep your cell on."

I shook my head. I couldn't believe how calm my voice was. "I'm going up the mountain, and I need you to do me a favor." I dug into the pocket of my jeans and pulled out a card. "Call this number for me."

Rick looked at the card and then at me. He looked back at the card, studying it. When he spoke, his voice and his face were somber. "Is everything okay, Raine?"

"No," I answered, swallowing hard. "But it will be if you'll make that call and tell him what I say."

I drove my SUV up the forest service road as far as I could before I was stopped by a good-sized oak across the trail. The higher I went, the thinner the smoke became, and after a while I was able to open the vents and lower the windows without choking. Families of deer darted across the road in front of me and frightened rabbits stood paralyzed in my headlights. Once, I saw two snakes scurrying for safety. All were headed for higher ground, like I was.

I got out and slipped on my backpack, then opened the back of the SUV. Cisco poked his head out, sniffed the air and sneezed. My hopes fell. Nothing could destroy a tracking dog's sense of smell quite as effectively as smoke. Still, there was a chance that we were high enough that the scent trail was still intact, so optimistically I snapped on Cisco's harness and let him jump out of the vehicle.

We walked another half mile or so to the end of the road, and by that time the pewter sky had lightened to patches of pale gray between the thick branches of overhanging limbs. The smell of smoke was infrequent now, more like that of a distant campfire than that of a roaring inferno. The canopy of green was so thick I could see nothing below me, not even the road where I had left my car. Beyond me and around me was a deep, dark cathedral of tall evergreens and pine-straw-covered floor.

I knelt down and brushed my fingers across the ground, Cisco's signal to begin tracking. "Track," I said. And then I added, though I can't say why, "Find the coyote."

Cisco sniffed the ground and then the air and started tracking to the east, into the sun. I followed his eager, waving tail and hoped I wasn't making the worst mistake of my life.

Cisco is trained to follow human scent, and although he has proven on more than one occasion to be easily distracted, I could predict with a fair degree of certainty that if he followed a trail, it was made by a human. Who that human might be was not quite as easy to guess, but under these circumstances the possibilities were limited.

Still, I couldn't stop thinking about the deer he had chased at tracking class, and the obedience commands he had refused to follow at the dog show, and I knew perfectly well that what he was trained to do and what he actually did when it counted were very often two different things. And I was trusting him to lead me through a forest fire to a man who had for fifteen years made a career out of not being found. I was obviously out of my mind.

I thought I had driven high enough above the fire line, but forest fires are tricky creatures and not easy to predict. We hadn't been hiking half an hour before the smoke began to thicken again, making my eyes water and my lungs bum. I could see flashes of undergrowth blazing and hear the sap sizzling in pine trees. I looked around, swiping my running eyes with my sleeve, for a clear path through the smoke. I didn't want Cisco breathing this. I didn't want to be breathing it either.

I called, "Cisco, here!" A lungful of smoke sent me into a coughing fit. Cisco, about ten feet ahead of me on the end of the lead, paused and wagged his tail uncertainly but made no move to return.

"Cisco!" I tugged on the lead, coughing, and he dug in his heels. He refused to move. "Damn it, Cisco, come here!"

He just stood there, tail held low and swishing slowly, and above the crackling of dried brush and the pop of sap, I thought I heard the high-pitched tone of an anxious whine.

I heard it before I saw it: the slow cracking, splintering, tearing sound of exploding wood. I dropped my hold on the leash. I screamed, "Cisco, run!" and I spun out of the way just as the flaming skeleton of a young pine crashed to the ground in front of me. Sparks soared toward the sky; heat flashed on my skin. I flung up an arm to shield my face and stumbled away. A hard blow to my shoulder knocked me forward and to my knees.

In another second, a huge, flaming branch stabbed the ground where I had been standing.

Cisco, looking worried and contrite, licked my smoke-smeared face. The cotton lead that trailed from his harness was on fire. I realized that he must have leapt over the flaming tree and pushed me out of the way just before the branch fell.

In my opinion, Lassie has ruined it for the dogs of this country. American pet owners expect every Lab, Rottie, Terrier and mixed breed who comes into their home to speak perfect English, detect gas leaks, fight off criminals and save their children from falling into hidden wells. No dog can live up to that. No sensible person would expect him to.

Until that moment I had been a sensible person. I expected my dogs to raid the trash, chase deer, get sprayed by skunks and lock me out of my own car. But I looked at Cisco, I looked at the flaming tree and at the branch that had almost impaled me, and suddenly Lassie seemed like a no-talent hack. I don't know how Cisco knew the branch was going to fall. Maybe he didn't. What made him leap over a flaming tree and knock me to my knees is anybody's guess. What I did know was that if he never earned an obedience title or ran another agility course or tracked anything other than rabbit or deer for the rest of his life, it wouldn't matter. He was my dog.

He was my hero.

With shaking fingers, I unsnapped the lead from his harness. Then I buried my face in his smoky fur while his whole body wiggled with rapturous tail wags and he covered my neck and chin with slobbery licks. I stayed that way until my rubbery knees felt strong enough to support me, and Cisco stood steady while I pulled myself to my feet.

"Come on, good boy," I said hoarsely, wrapping my fingers around his fur. "Let's get going."

We circled upward, out of the smoke, moving deeper and deeper into the woodland. Sometimes Cisco followed an eager zigzagging path that suggested he was on a scent trail. Sometimes he circled repeatedly where a pool of scent had settled and sometimes he dashed off in seemingly random directions. We dipped low into a valley where a haze of smoke had settled; we lost the trail. But as soon as we climbed out again, Cisco picked up a deer path. Head down, tail wagging, he began to track.

The thing about animal trails is that, barring natural disaster or a major shift in topography, they are pretty much immutable. Animals will follow the same path to a watering hole or a cave for generations. When pioneers first began exploring this country, they did so by following animal trails, which they knew were the shortest route between two points. Later those same animal paths became wagon trails, and wagon trails became paved roads, and paved roads became superhighways. Just a point of interest.

The trail that Cisco was following through the woods now, though faint and practically indiscernible to anyone who was not woods savvy, had probably been here for a hundred years. It led to a spot where water trickled out of the rocks and formed a clear, sweet pool underneath. It hadn't changed much from the time Andy and I had discovered it twenty-five years ago.

About a hundred yards from where I remembered the waterfall to be, Cisco's tail suddenly started wagging madly. He put his nose to the ground and raced toward a heavy-limbed sorghum tree. He circled the tree twice, then sat beneath it and barked, once.

Cisco's signal that he had found what he was tracking was to sit and to bark.

I stopped a few feet from the tree and murmured, "Good find, Cisco. Good boy."

Breathing slowly and cautiously, searching every inch of the woods that surrounded us with my eyes, I slipped the backpack off my shoulders and felt inside until I found Cisco's knotted rope toy, which was his reward for a good find. I tossed it to him, and he caught it happily in midair, then raced back over to me to begin chewing on his prize.

I took a breath, and another. And then a voice, sad and gentle and heartbreakingly familiar, said, "Hello, Rainbow."

The lower branches of the sorghum tree rustled and Andy Fontana leapt lightly to the ground.

I whispered, "Oh, Andy." And I ran into his arms.

Chapter Fourteen

When finally we released each other it was because Cisco was bumping at our knees, his whole body wagging as he proudly showed off his toy. Andy reached down and scratched Cisco behind the ears. "Quite a dog," he said. "I've been watching you the last mile or so. It was like somebody drew him a map."

"If you're a fugitive on the run," I said, "it's probably not a good idea to give a tracking dog a whole box of dog biscuits. Cisco will remember you for life now."

Andy glanced up at me with an eyebrow raised and said softly, "Ah."

He had changed; of course he had. His beard was full and lighter than I remembered; it took me a minute to realize that was because it was actually flecked with pale strands of gray. His hair was down to his shoulders and he had lost at least thirty pounds since I had last seen him. He was wearing army green twill pants and a multi-pocketed cotton jacket of the same material over a faded gray T-shirt. His boots were sturdy and well worn but still had plenty of service left in them. He looked like what he was, I suppose: a guerrilla.

He was older; so was I. But he was older in a way I didn't think I would ever be.

I said, unaccountably, "You stole my peanut butter."

"And a package of crackers and a box of toaster pastries. And half a plate of cookies. There wasn't much else except dog food. You don't go to a lot of trouble stocking your pantry, do you?"

"I thought Mischief ate the cookies."

For all that had changed about him, his eyes were the same, and when he smiled down at Cisco, then at me, it was as though the lifetime that had come between us had never been. He stuffed his hands into the pockets of his trousers and looked me over with that smile still in his eyes as he said, "So, you figured out it was me in your house that night. Who ratted me out, my buddy, here?" He nodded at Cisco, who had made himself comfortable on a patch of dried leaves and was once again chewing mightily on his toy.

"No, Cisco never finks on his friends. You shouldn't have messed with my dogs, Andy. Breaking into my house is one thing, but you shouldn't have opened Mischief's crate."

He nodded. "Yeah, I felt bad about that. I figured you kept her in there for a reason. But I couldn't be sure I'd put everything back where I found it, and I didn't want you to get suspicious, so I thought if you came home and found one of the dogs loose you'd blame it all on her."

The thing was, I believed him when he said he felt bad about it. My heart was pounding so hard it made my stomach hurt, but I believed him.

I said, "I did. I blamed it all on the dogs. It was a good plan."

Again he smiled. "Until I screwed up by waking up the whole kennel the next morning."

I frowned a little. "Yeah, what was that all about? Why didn't you just hightail it back up here? Didn't you know the FBI was probably watching the house?"

"That's what I wanted to find out. Apparently they weren't, because those hellhounds of yours made enough noise to wake the dead. I still think I would have been okay if it hadn't been for my good buddy, here." He shrugged a shoulder toward Cisco, who was happily oblivious. "He's the one that started all the barking. I guess he was looking for more dog biscuits."

"He thought you were a coyote."

Andy just smiled, then extended his hand to me. "You want to go sit by the waterfall for a minute?"

I should have said no. I should have at least insisted on taking my pack. There weren't any weapons in it, unless you count the Swiss Army knife, but there were supplies I might need in case...in case anything bad happened. But the truth is, I didn't think anything bad was going to happen. In fact, I was sure of it.

I said, "Cisco, with me," and I placed my hand in Andy's as Cisco, carrying his treasured toy in his mouth, came to my side.

Andy said, "I remember that dog Maude gave you when you came home after college—a golden retriever, wasn't it? Isn't that what this one is?"

I looked at him, startled. "How did you know

about that?"

He shrugged. "Just because I'm an international fugitive from justice doesn't mean I didn't keep up with goings-on back home. Anyway, I wasn't a fugitive back then. I was just a guy in love. I knew everything about you."

I guess that should have creeped me out, but it didn't. I said, "That dog's name was Cassidy. Cisco is her grandson."

We walked in silence for a while, our footsteps measuring with soft treads on the forest floor. Every step seemed to take us back in time, erasing suspicion, dread and mistrust. He was just Andy. I was just Raine.

He said, "Funny how things turn out. You run a kennel now. You train dogs. I never pictured it."

"I also work for the forest service," I pointed out.

"Yeah, but I always thought…"

He didn't finish, but I knew what he thought. He thought I'd be working for Greenpeace by now, or Save the Whales, or that I'd be leading ecological tours through the Amazon rain forest.

"I'm still trying to save the world, Andy," I said quietly. "I'm just doing it four paws at a time."

He surprised me by slipping his arm around my shoulders and drawing me to him in a swift, one-armed embrace. "Good for you, sweetheart," he said. "Good for you."

He kept his arm around my shoulders, and I was glad. After a time he said, "I was sorry to hear about your folks. They were—like icons, around here, and they were awfully good to me. I don't see how the community can be the same without them."

That was such a sweet thing to say. It made my throat thick. "Life goes on," I said. "Without you, or me…life goes on."

"I guess. But it changes."

"Yes." There was nothing I could add to that.

Because of the drought, the waterfall was less than a trickle, more like a wet veil that slid down the rock face. But a nice pool had formed in the moss at the base, and Cisco made a beeline for it, starting to lap up the water.

I said sharply, "Cisco, no!" and my dog looked at me sheepishly, then returned to my side.

The water might look clean, but I knew there was giardia and leptospirosis, and even up here you never knew what people had dumped in the streams. I tried never to let my dogs drink from a pool of standing water.

Andy was already shaking his head. "Hell of a thing," he said, "when a dog can't even drink out of a stream without risking his life."

I watched as Andy stepped across the small pool, reached behind the juncture in the rocks and pulled out his backpack. I knew then, if I had not already been certain, where he had hidden the diamonds all these years.

He opened his canteen and poured a measure of water into a field cup for Cisco. "Purified," he assured me.

Cisco drank his fill, then went in search of his toy, which he had dropped. I sat on the ground near the pool, and Andy sat beside me. Cisco found his toy and brought it over to us, flopping down on the ground to enjoy it.

"So. What was the key to?" I asked.

He hesitated only a moment. "You remember that old strongbox I used to have? I kept souvenirs and stuff from home in it. Later...I kept other things in it."

I nodded. "But you had your own key to that."

"Lost it." He slanted me a wry look. "I've been traveling a little." He shrugged and added, "I guess I could have smashed it open, but it seemed as easy to steal the key as to steal a hammer."

I nodded. Diamonds would be a lot easier to hide and transport in their loose form than secured in a bulky metal strongbox. "So you broke into the house to get the key from my charm bracelet. And the key worked, after all these years?"

He smiled. "Like a charm."

I couldn't help smiling back, just a little. There had always been something about Andy that could make me do that, even at the worst of times.

And then my brow knit in curiosity. "But why the phone call? Why did you leave the ringtone on my answering machine? You knew the FBI would be tracing calls made from stolen phones."

He shrugged. "Wouldn't have done them any good. I ditched the phone as soon as I used it, and they already knew where I was—they just couldn't find me." The familiar quirk of his mouth, a half-raised eyebrow. "Anyway, I called mostly to make sure you were really out of the house. And when I found the ringtone ... sorry, I couldn't resist."

I watched Cisco chewing contentedly awhile, then said, quietly, "I always thought you were innocent. All these years."

Andy took my hand. He held it in his open palm so that I could withdraw it if I wished. I did not. With his gaze on my hand, he said, "I was." He stroked my fingers, and I knew he noticed the lack of a wedding band. "I was innocent. Oh, maybe not of the crimes they accused me of, but innocent just the same."

Then, finally, he looked at me. "There weren't supposed to be any people in that chemical plant that night. It was Memorial Day, for Christ's sake." His fingers tightened in a swift, almost convulsive movement, then loosened. "No one was supposed to be there."

With those words, a decade of regrets, what-ifs and might-have-beens flashed between us, and I felt my heart slowly break in two.

I nodded, understanding. "But people were there. And they died."

"Yeah." A long, heavy breath. Again, he wouldn't look at me. "I had a lot of anger as a kid. I don't think you ever knew that. Later, the anger kind of needed a reason, so I gave it a noble name and a flag to hide behind. It was a head rush too, I won't lie about it, to have that kind of power, to do the things we—I mean I—did. After the bombing...hell, it was just survival. And when you're fighting to survive, you do things that you maybe wouldn't ordinarily do, you see things in a way you wouldn't ordinarily see them and you get involved with people ... well, there's just no way out."

I said firmly, "There's always a way out, Andy."

Once again he met my eyes. "I don't want you to think I'm trying to play the victim. I've done things; I don't deny that. There's a lot of crap going on in this world. Somebody needs to do something about it, and that's a fact. It's just that after a while, the things that have to be done about it seem...I don't know."

"More than one man should have to do," I volunteered softly.

"Yeah. I guess."

I couldn't help sliding my eyes toward his pack. He just smiled.

"After all these years...why now? Why did you come back now?"

"Did you know you can get the Hansonville Chronicle on the Internet now? Or most of it, anyway. Who would have ever thought it, huh? That's how I've been able to keep up with things, more or less, over the past couple of years. So I read about that development they were putting in on Hawk Mountain. Jeez, can you believe that? We used to play Daniel Boone fighting the Indians right there where they're planning to put the helipad, at least according to the plans they published."

Again a shrug of the shoulders. He reached down and picked up a twig, then snapped it in two. "There've been other times when I could have come back, when I could've made a deal like the one I'm working on now. The money alone never seemed worth the risk, you know? But now...I don't know. In a couple of years this land won't be the same as when I grew up. You won't be able to climb up here without tripping over the damn Yankees with their Abercrombie and Fitch hiking sticks and their silk sleeping bags...remember how we used to laugh at them? The waterfall will be gone..."

"And so will your hiding place," I said softly.

"Yeah," he admitted. "But mostly I came back now because I wanted to see it all one more time. To say good-bye."

"And you thought burning down half the national forest would be a good way to do that?"

He made one small sound of suppressed laughter and shook his head. "Don't play that with me, Raine. Your guys have got it under control and I made sure they'd be able to. Think of it as a controlled burn. The forest service would have had to do that sooner or later anyway, to control the undergrowth and revitalize the soil. And with so much of their natural habitats being bulldozed away, the wildlife would be finding it harder and harder to forage this summer. The fire is going to clear paths for them to higher ground, create natural deadfalls for shelter...well, you know the drill."

I didn't know why I should be surprised. He had taken the same courses I had; he had studied the same subjects. Only he had always been so much better at it. And that was only one of the reasons I was so angry.

I had to clench my fists hard at my sides to steady my voice. "You can't control a forest fire, Andy. This is yearling season. A six-week-old fox can't outrun a fire, and neither can a cougar cub or a nest of baby squirrels caught in a blazing tree. For every animal you might have saved from starvation, you've just killed two today."

He regarded me steadily. "It's the circle of life, babe."

"I don't know you anymore. I'm not sure I ever did."

He lifted his hand and touched me gently on

the cheek. His eyes were the saddest I have ever seen.

"Yeah," he said, "you did. Once."

There was something in his voice, in his face or maybe just in the touch of his hand that made me understand what I had been refusing to see before. I was very good at deceiving myself when I very much did not want to believe something. I had deceived myself into believing in Andy's innocence. I had deceived myself into believing there was no stolen treasury. I had even deceived myself into believing Andy would never come back here. And for as long as I possibly could, I had deceived myself about why he had come back. But I couldn't do that anymore.

Andy Fontana had wanted me to find him. He had waited for me to find him. He had stood in the shadow of my security lights for long, deliberate minutes, and he had set this fire so that I could find him.

I tried to breathe slowly. "You're making it look like you plan to use the smoke for cover, to get off the mountain."

"Right you are. I left this trail open, so while everybody is scrambling around down below I could just sneak on out behind them."

"Is that what you stole from the Feed and Seed? Matches?"

He didn't flinch. "Accelerant."

"You should have known I'd recognize the trail."

"Well, what can I say? It was a chance I had to take."

"I don't think so." My voice was a little unsteady. "I don't think you had to take this chance at all. I don't think you had to take a chance calling my phone or breaking into my house or setting off the security lights and waking all the dogs just to leave that silly sticker on my car. You could have been in and out of here in a day, Andy. Or you could have hidden out for months and no one would have known. You've been taking crazy chances since you got here. It's like you want to be caught."

He smiled dryly and tweaked my nose lightly with his forefinger. "You always were a lot smarter than you gave yourself credit for." And then the smile left his face and he looked away from me, out into the woods. "It all made sense when I started out. But being back here...made everything different. It's like part of my soul is buried here, you know? The part that used to care about things, that knew the difference between right and wrong...maybe the only part worth saving."

Then he looked at me. "You're my only connection to that part of me, Raine. You're the only one in this world who remembers the man I used to be. The kid I used to be. I had to see you one more time, just to make sure that the person I was ever really existed."

"I think he still exists," I insisted. "Somewhere deep inside, I think the man I knew is still alive. And it's not too late to save him." Desperation was rising in me, and it showed in my voice. Cisco looked up from his toy. "All these years you've been so smart, you've been so careful, and now to do something like this...you don't have to, Andy! We can figure it out."

He looked at me sadly, almost as though he

wanted to believe me. "Honey, the people I'm involved with...they're real bad guys. At first it seemed like a simple enough plan, but I'm in so far over my head now, there isn't any way out. I never wanted it to go this far. Sometimes I lie awake at night wondering how I got to this point. It wasn't anybody's fault but my own. And now I have to get myself out of it."

Long before he finished speaking I was shaking my head. "Turn yourself in," I said. "It's not you they want; it's the diamonds. You've got negotiating power. You can cut a deal."

If he was surprised by my mention of the diamonds he didn't show it He simply smiled. "Still the judge's daughter, aren't you? Yeah, I guess I could work a deal, but I'm not sure it would be the kind of deal I could live with. I wouldn't last a week in prison, Raine. And I can't think of a worse way to go."

"Then stay here." I couldn't believe I was saying it, but suddenly my mind was filled with Andy, the old Andy, the sweet, funny, irrepressible Andy who once saved a chicken from execution and who asked forgiveness from the trout before he ate it for dinner. I leaned toward him urgently. "You could live here in the forest forever; you know you could. It's where you belong; it's where you were happiest; it's where you'll be free." I gripped his hand. "There are a thousand places you can hide. No one ever has to know. Just leave the pack with me. I'll tell them I found it. Walk away, Andy, just walk away."

I didn't realize tears were streaming down my face until he caught one on the tip of his finger. He ran a gentle, comforting hand over the top of my head, caressing my neck. "I don't belong here anymore, sweetie. I've changed, and so has this place. The dozers are coming, the trucks, the condos—not just here, but everywhere. There's no place left for a man like me. This isn't my home anymore," he added sadly. "But it sure was a nice place to grow up." He ran a light hand over my hair. "Seeing you again makes it easier to say good-bye."

He reached for his pack and he stood up. "You'll be okay if you go back the way you came. The big guy here looks like he knows how to get you there." Andy leaned down and tugged at one of Cisco's ears. Cisco grinned up at him. "The fire won't get this high," Andy assured me. "They've already started cutting a fire break on the other side of Little Man Rock. I saw them through my binoculars. It's under control now. It'll be completely out by sundown."

I choked on the words and the tears in my throat "Andy, the FBI has blocked off the trail. You can't get out."

He just smiled. "I know that. I saw them through my binoculars too."

I struggled to my feet. "Please, just leave me the pack."

"Can't do that, sweetie. There might be something in it I need."

I clutched his arm. "Don't do this," I whispered. "You have a chance to make things right. Don't do this."

His eyes went very serious. He cupped my face in his two hands and said, "I am making things right, Rainbow. I want you to remember that okay? I'm making things right the only way I know how."

Then he kissed me, sweetly, tenderly. He smiled when he looked at me again, that same old smile that could always melt my heart. He dropped his hands from my face. "Love ya."

He turned and started walking down the trail.

I didn't hear the gunfire, which was a blessing, I guess. I would have had nightmares about it for the rest of my life. Later Uncle Roe told me that Andy had walked into the FBI ambush as though he knew it was there, and instead of halting when ordered to do so, he pulled a .44-caliber weapon from the back of his belt. The assault team responded as they had been trained to do.

Later they discovered several small film canisters filled with diamonds in Andy's backpack, and a box of ammunition that he had neglected to load into his gun. They call it suicide-by-cop.

The FBI reconnaissance team found me a couple of hours later, sitting by the waterfall where Andy had left me, weeping silently into my upraised knees while Cisco tried to lick the tears from my cheeks. They didn't have to tell me it was all over. I already knew.

I think I must have known from the moment I heard Andy had come back.

Chapter Fifteen

The fire smoldered, burying our mountain valley in ugly gray smoke for days. People complained about deer on their porches and foxes in their gardens and snakes in their basements. No laundry was hung on the line and windows were closed up tight despite the sweltering heat.

Rick said I could take some time off if I needed to, but how could he spare me? Besides, I needed to be outdoors; I needed to be working; I needed to save something.

So when I wasn't checking the service roads and watching for spot flare-ups, taking water samples or writing reports, I was out there with a shovel and an ax with the rest of the guys, cutting back deadfalls and clearing debris from the hiking trails. In terms of all forest fires, this one had caused minimal damage, and Rick actually observed one day when he was in an optimistic mood that it had saved us the trouble of a controlled burn later in the year.

I came home exhausted every night, covered in

blisters and soot, tasting ashes in my mouth, to be greeted by a household filled with wagging tails and happy, expectant eyes. My dogs didn't care that I was so filthy I had to leave my boots on the back porch and wash off my face and arms with a hose before I even came inside. They were as ecstatic to see me as if I had been covered in liver paste. Coming home was the best part of my day.

It always had been.

The FBI questioned me for a few hours on Sunday, right after everything happened, but it was just routine. They knew everything I did, and what they didn't know, I told them. Sonny Brightwell actually came down, looking important enough in her Armani suit and silver-clasped briefcase to impress even the FBI, and insisted upon being present during the interview. I don't know who called her, but I was glad she was there. Not because I needed a lawyer, but because she made them let me bring Cisco into the interview room with me, and keep him there the whole time. At one point she even had six agents scurrying around to find a bowl for my dog to drink from, and insisted that someone bring him a canine protein bar from my backpack. After his snack, Cisco settled down on the floor at my feet for a nice, long nap. I think that was when I started to realize we were both going to be okay.

Afterward, Sonny tried to apologize again for what had happened at the dog show, but there was no need. We both knew that by dissociating herself from me when she thought I might have been involved, even unintentionally, with ecoterrorism, she had only acted in the best interests of the people she had been hired to represent. Neither one of us suggested that I rejoin the board of Save the Mountains. Sometimes, after all, sacrifices have to be made for the greater good.

Buck left message after message on my answering machine, but I deleted them all. He came by the house a couple of times and left notes asking me to call, but I didn't.

Then the rains came.

A hard rain after a forest fire might have been disastrous, causing landslides, flooding and permanent soil erosion in the places where the ground cover had been burned away. But this was a nice, slow, misty rain that started in the morning and drizzled through the night and congealed into fog for a while before turning into rain again. It cleaned the air and soaked the ashes and drowned the embers that still smoldered hidden beneath debris. After a few days of this, people were complaining about the mud, but I could almost see the tiny seedlings beginning to push their way up through the scorched surface of the forest floor.

On Friday morning I asked Uncle Roe to meet me for breakfast at Miss Meg's Cafe. I was wearing my forest service uniform underneath my rain slicker, which made me look somewhat official. I spotted Dexter Franklin dining alone at a booth, just as he did most mornings, reading the paper, and I pointed him out to Uncle Roe. The two of us made our way over to him and slid into the booth opposite him.

"Morning, Mr. Franklin," I said. "Do you mind if we join you?"

He looked annoyed; then, when he noticed Uncle Roe, his expression became more guarded. "Miss Raine," he said, looking from one of us to the other. "Sheriff. What can I do for you?"

"I'm just here to have a cup of coffee," said Uncle Roe, signaling for the waitress.

"And I'm here following up on your complaint about the bear that damaged your truck," I added.

His features relaxed some, though he still looked nervous. "Well, it's about damn time. I phoned that in a week ago."

"We've had our hands full."

He grunted and waited until the waitress had taken our order for two coffees before he said, "Hell of a thing, that fire. I lost three guineas and a half dozen baby ducks. Choked to death."

"I'm sorry to hear that."

"My wife's pretty upset. She set a store by her guinea hens."

"It was quite a mess," I agreed.

"Well, that's what you get, bringing in a bunch of damn Mexicans, can't even read English. Next thing you know they're burning the damn county down."

I blinked at him. "I'm sorry?"

He thumped the newspaper in his hand. "That's what it says right here. That the fire started when those Mexican workers that contract foreman brought in started burning brush without a permit."

The first two pages of the local paper had, of course, been covered with the story of the "shoot-out on the mountain," but people had been talking about that event all week and interest in it had pretty much worn thin. Like people everywhere, the residents of Hanover County were mostly interested in the things that directly affected their lives. Similarly, the death of an international fugitive and suspected terrorist had been hot news around the nation for twenty-four hours, but once the story was told, it was told, and other news soon grabbed the headlines. For security reasons, no mention was ever made of the diamonds. Likewise, Sonny had suggested to those in charge that there was nothing to be gained by mentioning my involvement in the case, and they had agreed.

That was probably what I was most grateful to Sonny for.

"The paper sometimes gets things wrong," I pointed out to Dexter Franklin.

He grunted and took a sip of his coffee.

The waitress brought my coffee and Uncle Roe's, and when she was gone I added, "For example, they got that whole thing wrong last week about the bear at the construction site."

The wariness returned to his eyes, just for a minute; then he laughed. "Now that's where you're wrong, little missy. They had pictures of that one, damn bear in a pickup truck, right there on the front page."

I nodded, lifting my coffee cup. The coffee was still too hot to drink. "But a bear didn't slash the tires on all those dump trucks, or take a crowbar to the Bobcat."

His eyes narrowed as I went on. "What I figure happened was, somebody was up there at the site, trying to make a little mischief for the construction crew while they were at supper. Maybe that somebody had a grudge against the contractor and a little too much to drink, I don't know. And then the bear came down out of the woods, sniffing around the pickup. The pickup was parked way on the other side of the dump trucks, so there's a good chance the bear might not have even noticed the person, whoever he was, who was fooling around with the equipment. Or maybe he was just so hungry he didn't care. At any rate, when that bear started roaring and complaining and trying to get at the food that was in the pickup, my guess is it probably scared the fellow pretty bad. He probably got in his own truck and got out of there as fast as he could." Dexter Franklin looked from me to Uncle Roe, but he said nothing.

"Or maybe," I said, watching him, "it wasn't the bear who interrupted the damage he was doing to the equipment. Maybe it was a man, and the bear came along later. Maybe this man startled the fellow, or tried to stop him, and they had a fight. Maybe the fellow with the crowbar took a swing at the other guy, might even have hurt him, and when he tried to run away the guy chased him down the road in his pickup and ran him over."

Franklin said fiercely, "What the hell are you talking about, woman?"

"Or maybe," I added, "he didn't really mean to hit the man at all, just scare him, and maybe he would have even stopped, and tried to see if he was okay, but he was afraid to. Because if he had stopped, somebody might have noticed and wondered what he was doing—somebody like a truckload of construction workers who were coming up the road about that time, to pick up one of the crew and take him back to the hotel."

"They said they were almost run off the road by a white Ford truck going the opposite way," said Uncle Roe mildly, stirring a third sugar packet into his cup. "What color's your truck again, Dex?"

Dexter Franklin frowned mightily, "What the hell are you getting at, Roe? Half the trucks in this county are Fords, and the other half are white."

"True enough," agreed Uncle Roe. He tasted his coffee. "But not all of them have fender damage on the right front side."

"I told you, a bear did that—"

"You only decided a bear did it after you read the story in the paper," I pointed out. "You were driving your wife's car that Thursday morning because the front of your truck had exactly the kind of damage the police were looking for. Your truck was parked over ten miles away from Valley Street, and bears don't roam that wide a territory. And I don't think any of us are ready to believe that there's an organized gang of bears out there with a vendetta against pickup trucks. It didn't happen, Dexter."

His eyes blazed at me, but I noticed he had gone a little white around the lips. "Are you calling me a liar, missy?"

"If you call me 'missy' one more time, I'll be doing worse than that. A bear didn't pry the fender half off your truck, Dexter. You did, trying to hide the damage because you were afraid if you took it to a body shop the police would find out. The paper said that all garages and repair shops had been asked to notify the sheriff's department about any vehicles that came in with suspicious damage."

"Well, I've heard about all of this I'm going to take." Dexter Franklin stood abruptly. His face was bright red, with purple veins glowing in his nose and cheeks. His eyes were furious. "You need to be careful who you're accusing of what, young lady, if you don't want to wind up in a court of law. And you." He thrust a finger at my uncle's face. Never a good idea. "If you want to keep that shiny badge of yours—"

The bell over the door tinkled, and Buck came in. He just stood beside the door, his hands resting lightly on his utility belt, and watched us. Dexter couldn't miss it.

Uncle Roe said politely, "Sit down, Dexter" He picked up his coffee cup. "I've got a team of deputies out at your place right now with a search warrant, looking for a crowbar. You want to save us some trouble and tell me where it's at?"

Slowly, Dexter Franklin sat down. His red face was now covered with a light mist of perspiration, and when he linked his fingers around his coffee cup, they were shaking. He looked down at the table, at the wrinkled newspaper spread across it, at the remains of his breakfast. Anyone observing him might have thought he was praying. Maybe he was.

Then he said, hoarsely, "It was the bear. The goddamn bear. Came around the side of that big dump truck and 'bout scared me to death. I was backing up, trying to get out of the way, and there was that Mexican. I just swung the crowbar, don't know why. Just spooked, not thinking right. I didn't mean to hurt him. But I knew I had to get out of there before somebody else came, and there was the damn bear... I got in the truck and I floored it. Hell, I didn't know that Mex was running down the side of the road. It was near dark, and I guess I'd had a couple of beers, and then...well, how did I know what I'd hit?" The thing was, a jury would probably believe him. Uncle Roe stood up. "Let's go on down to the office, Dex. We can talk about it some more there."

Slowly, Dexter Franklin stood up and joined my uncle beside the table. "By the way," Uncle Roe told him, "his name was Manuel Rodriguez. We finally got hold of his family. He had a wife and three children back in Mexico."

"And a dog," I added quietly.

My uncle Roe is a good sheriff and a nice guy. He did not embarrass a prominent citizen like Dexter Franklin by cuffing him or making it look like he was being escorted out of the cafe. Besides, what would have been the point? He knew where Dexter lived and could have picked him up at any time. Buck stood by the door and let them pass, so that it might look to any of the diners who noticed that he had just come in to see me.

Maybe he had.

Buck walked out into the misty morning with me, and we watched Dexter get into the patrol car with Uncle Roe. Buck said, "Good work. We might have let this one slip past us, what with"— only a slight hesitation— "everything else going on. But you kept at it. Thanks."

I took a deep breath of the clean, rain-washed air and flipped my hood over my hair. "What do you expect from me?" I replied. "I'm a judge's daughter."

I stepped from the shelter of the awning and into the street. Things were quieter now, what with the FBI packed up and gone, and construction shut down because of the rain. There was hardly any traffic on the street, and our town was almost back to normal.

I turned back to Buck. "By the way," I said, "it was you. It was always you."

Buck's tired eyes smiled, and he came out into the rain to open my car door for me. As I drove off I could still see him in the rearview mirror, standing in the rain, watching after me.

Chapter Sixteen

Experts say the Garden of Eden was located in the Middle East somewhere. Personally, I've always suspected it was right here, in the heart of the Smoky Mountains.

There is such an extravagance of life here, such a determined, fecund, unlimited bounty of possibilities. Hope bursts forth like tangled vines, wrapping itself around tree stumps and fence posts and utility poles and every incursion of modem man, whether you want it to or not.

Some people have speculated that the cure for every disease known to humankind might be found in the deep green jungles of a Smoky Mountain woodlands. I don't know about that, but I do know that healing seems to occur faster here. Before the summer was over almost all evidence of the fire had been erased, leaving in its wake smooth forest floor and lush new growth. Squirrels returned to their nests, foxes to their caves. Deer and bear found plenty to nibble on in the higher elevations and left the humans' gardens alone. It was almost as though our mountains had been around so long that they were surprised by nothing. They knew how to recover from whatever life threw at them, and they wasted no time getting on with it.

Sometime in the middle of the summer Maude came into the office while I was working at the computer and tossed a flyer on my desk. "Super Paws Agility Club is having a preseason trial," she said. "Indoors, air-conditioned. You want to go?"

I looked up. "AKC?"

She nodded.

I started filling out the entry form.

I really don't know why I took Cisco, except that, since the fire, we'd pretty much been inseparable. And because Sonny said, "He misses running and jumping. He likes all the sounds and smells at a trial. He really wants to go." Okay, it was silly, but sometimes I get sentimental about things like that.

However, I hadn't trained with Cisco all summer and it would have been a waste of money to enter him in anything. He was just along for the ride. This was Mischief's shot at the title, and I felt bad about her having missed her chance to run in June.

This was a dedicated all-breed agility trial, and no other competitions were taking place under the big, domed roof. There were no big tents displaying unique dog items, just a couple of T-shirt vendors and an action photographer. The concession stand sold hamburgers and tuna sandwiches. And the huge, echoing building was full to bursting with agility enthusiasts who hadn't had a chance to compete in more than six weeks.

Two rings were going at once, and Maude and I found a spot between them, which wasn't easy to do. We set up our collapsible mesh crates and our camp chairs on the artificial turf not far from the bleachers where family and friends could watch and cheer on their favorite dogs. I saw quite a few people I knew—the same crowd usually traveled the circuit—and a lot of them had been at the trial in June. They waved and greeted me as if nothing had changed. And in the world of dogs, it hadn't.

In absolutely no time, I was in the swing of things again. I had a couple of hours to kill before it was my turn to run with Mischief, so I enjoyed watching the other classes compete. Maude ran Rune, her beautiful female, in the Open class, and came in fourth. It was a perfect run, clean and fast, but there were three border collies in her division. How could a regular dog compete with that?

I took Mischief over the practice jump to warm her up, and because Cisco looked so dejected, watching from behind the zippered door of his crate, I let him take the jump a few times too. Afterward I zipped Cisco back in his crate and took Mischief over to the gate area to wait our turn.

I was feeling pretty confident about our chances as I watched the other competitors. The course wasn't all that difficult and there were no abrupt pivots that might put stress on my knee, which I had wrapped tightly just in case. Mischief had been working hard the last couple of weeks, and I had confidence she could do it. We were ready.

Vaguely I heard Cisco barking in the

background, and when I looked over the heads of the other competitors I could see him pawing furiously at the mesh door of his crate. I opened my mouth to shout at him, but just then the gate steward called, "Mischief on deck!" and it was our turn.

I took off Mischief's lead and tossed it aside, put her in a stay at the start line and walked to the second jump. Mischief, bright eyed, waited for me to give her the signal. I raised my hand and...

Suddenly a gold blur shot past Mischief, over the first two jumps and through the tunnel. Someone shouted, "Loose dog!"—too little, too late—and Mischief bounded over the two jumps and into the tunnel, thundering after the troublemaker.

I remember hearing a cheer from the bleachers: "Woo-hoo! Go, Cisco, run!" and when I whirled around, there was Buck, standing and punching the air with his fist with the same kind of untrammeled enthusiasm that's usually reserved for a quarterback who's about to the make the winning touchdown of the season. I also recall, as though in slow motion, noticing a hole in the mesh of Cisco's crate door the approximate size and shape of the one he had left in my screen door a couple of months before. But for the most part I just stood there, disbelieving, until Cisco emerged from the tunnel, streaked past me, and sailed over the next jump.

I started to shout, "Damn it, Cisco!" but the words never left my mouth. I had never seen anything like it. The dog was a rocket. Of course he avoided the obstacles that would have slowed him down—the A-frame; the dog-walk, which he hated; and he leapt over the seesaw instead of walking on it—but he shot through the tire jump, flew across the broad jump and blurred through the weave poles like they were melting. Mischief was left so far behind that she would not have been able to catch him if she'd had the rest of the day. The judge was frantically blowing her whistle, the audience was shrieking with laughter and Buck was shouting from the stands, "Go, Cisco!"

I just stood there, laughing so hard that I could hardly gasp out the words, "Run, boy, run!"

Later I learned that the electronic timers revealed that Cisco had run a 54-second course in 27.3 seconds— surely a world record, even if he did take a few shortcuts. Unfortunately for Cisco, in this particular game you can win only if you play by the rules. But I guess he thought it was worth it, to get his point across.

Sometimes, I suppose, it is.

By the time I snapped the leash back on Mischief, thanked the judge and even—because how I could resist?— made a small curtsy to the laughing crowd, Cisco had leapt the ring gating and raced back to his crate, where he was waiting for me with a foolish grin on his face. Maude stood beside the crate with her arms crossed, trying to look stem, her eyes brimming with amusement.

"You made a couple of mistakes out there," she commented, because it was our habit to critique each other's performance in the ring.

"Ah, gee, do you think?"

"First, you lost control of your dog. Second, you really need to spend some time working on

Mischief's start-line stay..."

I shook my head, exhausted with laughter, as I zipped Mischief back into her crate. "Where is Cisco's leash?"

She handed it to me. I was just snapping it on Cisco's collar when Buck said behind me, "Nice run, champ."

There was a part of me that still felt uncomfortable around him, awkward and hurt and closed off—just like there was a part of me that couldn't stop thinking about things, late at night, that were better off put away forever. I was trying, but healing is a process that takes its own time.

I said, "Thanks. But I didn't do anything."

"I meant Cisco."

Of course he did.

"What are you doing here, anyway?" I asked.

"Maude mentioned the trial. I had the day off, so I thought I'd drive over."

"But Cisco isn't even competing."

"Guess you should have mentioned that to him."

I couldn't help smiling. "Well, that explains it, then. He put on that show just for you."

Buck said, "Buy you a burger?"

"Are you talking to me or Cisco?"

"Both."

We walked over to the concession stand with Cisco between us and ordered two greasy hamburgers, a couple of soft drinks and a bowl of water. We sat at a plastic table and Cisco, having finished his water, settled

down hopefully at Buck's feet.

"Don't you dare feed that dog hamburger," I

warned him. "He has not been a good dog."

"I wouldn't do that," Buck assured me, unwrapping his burger. "It's got onions."

But even as I watched, he carefully removed the onions from a broken-off corner of the burger and slipped it under the table to Cisco. I lobbed a balled-up paper napkin at him, which he dodged.

It had been a long time since we'd been together like this.

There is something about a dog show that makes even the worst food taste good, and I enjoyed every bite of the hamburger. We sat for a while, watching the action in the ring that we could see, while Cisco snoozed under the table. I played with the straw in my drink. Then I said, because it had to be said, "I owe you an apology."

He turned his gaze back to me. Quiet eyes, strong eyes, good eyes.

"What I said to you, about you being the reason the FBI made the connection to Andy all those years ago—it wasn't true, and it wasn't fair. They already knew it was him. You just gave them another piece of the puzzle."

Buck picked up his drink and put it down again. He said quietly, "Andy was my friend too, you know."

I nodded. "I know. I don't think I ever thought about it much before but…I know."

"Maybe if we had talked more…back then…"

And I said, "I know."

It was hard to hold eye contact with him, for reasons I didn't entirely understand, and I shifted my gaze back to the ring, where a black lab was just spoiling a perfect run by knocking over the bar on the last jump. The handler threw up her hands in dismay, then hurried to catch up with her dog and tell him how wonderful he was. In the world of dogs, even when they make a mistake, you don't stop loving them.

Buck said, "Are you ever going to tell me what happened that day on the mountain?"

I looked back at him. "It's all in the report. I told the FBI everything."

His gaze was calm and steady. "I mean what's not in the report. I mean what happened with you, inside."

"Yeah," I said after a moment, and my voice sounded softer. I felt softer. "I'll tell you. Someday."

Someday came sooner than I thought it would. And that was when the healing began.

The construction on Valley Street wound to a close as the utility lines were laid and the equipment was moved out, just in time for autumn leaf season. The Save the Mountains group did a good job of convincing the contractor it would be in his best interest to hydroseed and put in a few soil-preserving plants before pulling out, and in a couple of years the ugly scar across the face of the mountain would not be quite so noticeable.

As for the bear, the rest of the summer passed peacefully without another sighting. As the drought ended and the leaves and berries that were his natural diet came into season, he probably found plenty to eat in the woods. Or perhaps the fire pushed him higher into the mountains, where the hunting was better.

Well, I should say, almost no more sightings were made of the bear. The strangest thing happened one dawn late in September. I was awakened by the sound of Cisco's low, guttural growling. I could see him in the gray light, standing at the closed bedroom door with his tail straight up and his ears pricked, staring hard at the door.

I slipped out of bed in my nightshirt and crept downstairs as silently as possible, my heart pounding. Cisco pressed himself to my side in a perfect heel position that I would never see from him inside the obedience ring. I checked the windows. Nothing. I eased open the front door, trying not to wake the other dogs, and peeked outside. Cisco poked his nose through the door, sniffed the damp misty air, and growled again. I said, "Shh…" and stepped silently out onto the front porch, my fingers wrapped reassuringly around Cisco's collar.

The morning was cool and damp, and I rubbed one bare foot against my leg as I stepped onto the cold boards of the porch. I saw nothing. My skin prickled and I shivered a little, turning to go inside. Then Cisco growled again, and I stopped.

The bear was standing in the driveway not twenty feet away, half wrapped in mist, as still as a statue. It had to be the same bear who had wedged himself into the cab of that pickup early in the summer. How could there be two bears that size on this mountain?

He was still the most magnificent creature I had ever seen. Even in the pale light of dawn, the planes of his muscular form, the thick rough coat of blue-black fur, were evident. He had legs the size of small tree trunks and paws as big as dinner plates. I could hear him huffing air in and out as he smelled us, and I caught my breath. Cisco stiffened and I got a firmer grip on his collar.

Then the bear turned its head and looked at me. I could see the reflection of ambient light in his black eyes, just a glint, and for some reason it reminded me of a repressed grin. He stood there for as long as I could hold my breath, just gazing at me, and then he turned and began to amble across the yard, back toward the woods.

There was enough light by now for me to see him pause as he reached the wood line, and he actually looked back over his shoulder toward the house. I had the craziest notion that he was saying good-bye...or maybe, thank you.

Then he broke into a lope and started up the hill. I could hear small branches break as he crashed into them, and I smiled, whispering, "Run, big fellow. Run. Run on home."

I was still standing there, smiling, when the screen door creaked softly behind me, and Buck, in T-shirt and boxers, came out. "What's up?" he asked, slipping his arms around my waist.

I released Cisco's collar and sank back against Buck, soaking up his good male scent and his tousled, just- from-bed warmth. "Nothing," I said. "Just watching the sun rise."

We are not back together. Both of us are certain about that. But we'll never really be apart either. And there's no harm in being reminded, now and then, that we've made the right choice.

"Well, will you look at that," Buck murmured, resting his chin on my head. "Isn't that something?"

At first I thought he had caught a glimpse of the bear, but in a moment I saw what he meant.

The rising sun, heating the damp foliage and evaporating fog, had formed a pale, perfect rainbow over the tops of the backlit evergreens that curved across the mountain.

"Yeah," I said, smiling again as I leaned my head back against Buck's shoulder. "It sure is."

But by the time I spoke the words, the rainbow was gone.

**

Also in The Raine Stockton Dog Mystery Series

SMOKY MOUNTAIN TRACKS

A child has been kidnapped and abandoned in the mountain wilderness. Her only hope is Raine Stockton and her young, untried tracking dog Cisco...

GUN SHY

Raine rescues a traumatized service dog, and soon begins to suspect he is the only witness to a murder.

BONE YARD

Cisco digs up human remains in Raine's back yard, and mayhem ensues. Could this be evidence of a serial killer, a long-unsolved mass murder, or something even more sinister... and closer to home?

SILENT NIGHT

It's Christmastime in Hansonville, N.C., and Raine and Cisco are on the trail of a missing teenager. But when a newborn is abandoned in the manger of the town's living nativity and Raine walks in on what appears to be the scene of a murder, the holidays take a very dark turn for everyone concerned.

THE DEAD SEASON

Raine and Cisco accept a job leading trouble teenagers on a winter wilderness hike, and soon find themselves trapped on a mountainside... with a killer.

HIGH IN TRIAL

A carefree weekend turns deadly when Raine and Cisco travel to the South Carolina low country for an agility competition.

Spine-chilling suspense by Donna Ball

SHATTERED

A missing child, a desperate call for help in the middle of the night... is this a cruel hoax, or the work of a maniacal serial killer who is poised to strike again?

NIGHT FLIGHT

She's an innocent woman who knows too much. Now she's fleeing through the night without a weapon and without a phone, and her only hope for survival is a cop who's willing to risk his badge—and his life—to save her.

SANCTUARY

They came to the peaceful, untouched mountain wilderness of Eastern Tennessee seeking an escape from the madness of modern life. But when they built their luxury homes in the heart of virgin forest they did not realize that something was there before them... something ancient and horrible; something that will make them believe that monsters are real.

EXPOSURE

Everyone has secrets, but when talk show host Jessamine's Cray's stalker begins to use her past to terrorize her, no one is safe ... not her family, her friends, her coworkers, and especially not Jess herself.

RENEGADE by Donna Boyd

Enter a world of dark mystery and intense passion, where human destiny is controlled by a species of powerful, exotic creatures. Once they ruled the Tundra, now they rule Wall Street. Once they fought with teeth and claws, now they fight with wealth and power. And only one man can stop them... if he dares.

Also by Donna Ball

The Ladybug Farm series by Donna Ball

For every woman who ever had a dream... or a friend

A Year on Ladybug Farm

At Home on Ladybug Farm

Love Letters from Ladybug Farm

Christmas on Ladybug Farm

Recipes from Ladybug Farm

Vintage Ladybug Farm

The Hummingbird House

Romance Revisited by Donna Ball

MATCHMAKER, MATCHMAKER

He was a cowboy looking for a wife. She was a lady specializing in brides. They were made for each other... They just didn't know it yet.

A MAN AROUND THE HOUSE

He was the answer to a busy working woman's dreams. But was he too good to be true?

FOR KEEPS

He's an animal trainer who lives by one rule: never get attached. She's a social worker who knows all too well the price of getting involved. It may take an entire menagerie to bring them together, but eventually they both must learn that sometimes it's for keeps.

STEALING SAVANNAH

He was a reformed jewel thief now turned security expert and her job depended on his expertise. But could he be trusted not to steal the most valuable jewel of all-- her heart?

UNDER COVER

She's working on the biggest case of her life, and her cover has already been blown-- by the very man she's investigating. Now they must work together to solve an even bigger mystery-- their future together.

THE STORMRIDERS

They were thunder and lightning when they were married, and their divorce has been no less turbulent. But trapped together during a deadly blizzard with the lives of an entire community depending on them, they discover what's really important, and that some storms are worth riding out.

INTERLUDE

Sometimes a chance encounter is over in a moment, and sometimes it can last a lifetime.

CAST ADRIFT

She was a marine biologist on short deadline to find a very important dolphin, with no time to waste on romance. He was a sailor who knew there could only be one captain on his ship-- himself. But two weeks at sea together could change everything...

ABOUT THE AUTHOR....

Donna Ball is the author of over a hundred novels under several different pseudonyms in a variety of genres that include romance, mystery, suspense, paranormal, western adventure, historical and women's fiction. Recent popular series include the Ladybug Farm series by Berkley Books and the Raine Stockton Dog Mystery series. Donna is an avid dog lover and her dogs have won numerous titles for agility, obedience and canine musical freestyle. She lives in a restored Victorian Barn in the heart of the Blue Ridge mountains with a variety of four-footed companions. You can contact her at http://www.donnaball.net.

CPSIA information can be obtained
at www.ICGtesting.com
Printed in the USA
LVHW011157110222
710694LV00005B/658

9 780985 774851